THE
MONSTERS
WE DESERVE

MARCUS SEDGWICK

ZEPHYR

First published in the UK in 2018 by Zephyr,
an imprint of Head of Zeus Ltd

9 7 5 3 1 2 4 6 8

A catalogue record for this book is available from
the British Library.

ISBN (HB): 9781788542302
ISBN (FTPB): 9781788548380
ISBN (E): 9781788542296

Designed by Jessie Price
Typeset by Adrian McLaughlin
Images © Marcus Sedgwick and Shutterstock

Printed and bound in Serbia by Publikum

Head of Zeus Ltd
5–8 Hardwick Street
London EC1R 4RG
WWW.HEADOFZEUS.COM

For MS

Wer mit Ungeheuern kämpft, mag zusehn, dass er nicht dabei zum Ungeheuer wird. Und wenn du lange in einen Abgrund blickst, blickt der Abgrund auch in dich hinein.

— *Friedrich Nietzsche*

W

And if you gaze long enough into an abyss, the abyss will gaze back into you. Who said that?

Up here there are abysses. Of all kinds.

Up here...

Five thousand feet of altitude. Ringing chasms on every side. Mountain torrents gushing icy waters through throats of rock; a white noise of oblivion. Outrageously uncountable trees, witness to everything, but mute. The air is thin, dry.

Wait.

Do you see that comma? No, listen, do you see that comma? It's there for a reason. I didn't write: the air is thin and dry. I didn't write: the air is thin. And dry.

I wrote: *The air is thin, dry.*

The comma is important – it's the single snatched breath, a moment of hanging in which you can hear my failing attempts to find the right way to explain all this.

So that's clear now? Good. One clear thing. And these little things are important. Something as small as a comma could turn out to be significant, perhaps vital. And you know, at this altitude, it often takes your brain a twinkling of time to find the right word. To think... lucidly.

Yes, there are endless abysses up here, and no doubt there is something in their depths. So far I have seen nothing, but maybe that's because I've been looking in the daytime.

Night-time, on the other hand, the night... The night is when monsters arrive, when monsters are made. But before we make anything, let me make one other thing understood – this will not be easy. It will not be straightforward. It will move in other ways, sideways and backways: ways we don't have words for. Something else: it has always struck me as troubling that the words in books are printed in black and white, when life is anything but. The binary colour of words on a page give the sense of simplicity and clarity. But life doesn't work like that. And neither should a good story. A good story ought to leave a little grey behind, I think.

I can't help any of this, but I undertake to do my best to set things down as well as I can, and after all, it seems that I am expected to.

You expect me to.

Once more, I have to rummage through the paintboxes and toolkits of my imagination in order to conjure some horror or other, and as you know, I have been unable to find anything of interest to work with.

And yet there is so much to choose from, so many monsters. I might think of Grendel, slain by Beowulf, who likewise dispatched Grendel's mother, far beneath the surface of the sea. Or the twisted beast, Caliban on his tempestuous island. *Be not afeard*, he said. *Be not afeard?* Be very afeard. There were three witches once in *a desert place*, inciting others to murder and malevolence: Lady Macbeth with blood on her hands. *Fair is foul and foul is fair.* Mr Hyde, the monster in Dr Jekyll, the *ordinary secret sinner*, the monster in all of us, the monster we all create ourselves. Count Dracula, the antihero many perhaps crave to be; sexual and immortal. *The blood is the life.*

So many monsters. *Once, they were as plentiful as berries in a pail, or blades of grass in the meadow.* Or the trees of an alpine forest. But are there fewer monsters than there used to be? A moment's thought and I will give you my answer to that.

Monsters lurk in every culture's life blood – the history of the world is as much the history of its monsters as its angels, and who is the more fascinating: Elizabeth Bathory and her blood-bathing, or Mother Teresa and her poor? Vlad Țepeș and his impalings, or Saint Francis and his birds? I wish I could give you better answers, I really do, but monsters throng about

us; they always have. That being the case, why am I not able to pull something out of the hat? Any one of these beasts has held our ghastly attention across decades, even many hundreds of years.

I would like to mention that you sent me here. It was your idea. *Go and immerse yourself. Maybe that will help.*

So here I am, and yes, the maps and the lines I drew on them were not your doing, but it is because of you that I'm here, groping around with my rusting creativity, trying to think how to bring a monster back to life. And, like it or not, I settled on one particular monster, after all. Though I really can't fathom why it's *this* monster I have chosen. For that's what you want, isn't it? Something you can unleash on the world, in just the way Mary did.

A monster brought to life.

E

What was it you said?

Something inspired by it, but not.

Something that's like it, but not.

You publishers never want much, do you? And what do I want? I want to get it done and come home. That's what I want. And not to suffer any casualties of war in the process.

It's beautiful here. And very, very quiet. You know I like those two qualities, crave them in fact, as you have often pointed out to me – how they are hidden (or not so hidden) in my books, despite what most people see in them. And what most people see in them is blood. For all your protestations, I worry that that's all you want to see too. I remember that conversation about my very first manuscript. *Give me blood*, you said. *Give me blood. Give me power.* The quietness isn't enough, is it? It never is. Yes, some approaching sense of foreboding will do, but what you really wanted was the blood. But of course, you never really know what a book is until it's finished, maybe until years after it's finished. Sometimes it takes that long to know what you were really writing. Do you know what I'm writing now? Do you know what this book will be? How can you, when I don't know it myself?

Beauty and silence. We alpine dwellers have plenty of those, but there's something else here that pleases me less, something I cannot put my finger on, but which I can sense is coming. It waits between the dark shadows, among the tree trunks of the forest. It tumbles off the mountain in frigid waters. It comes on the blowing of the wind, though that is rare enough here, something I wasn't expecting in the mountains. I expected grandeur; nature flung over the bones of the world. I got it. I expected solitude; I got that too, solitude without measure, if I want it. And I expected the winds to blow; but instead, the tight valley where I've been living provides shelter from all but the most accurately aligned breeze.

When I arrived, early October, I could have perhaps been forgiven for mistaking it for summer. The colour of the leaves of some trees was turning, but alongside the occasional beech and birch, larch and oak, most of the trees are the endless armies of firs, looming sentinels on the mountainside, silent, all-seeing.

Firs. Evergreens. Ever greens. That fooled me. The sun fooled me. The blue skies fooled me. The air itself fooled me. It has been really hot. But, once or twice now; a sudden drop in the temperature and the air has changed its smell. *Something* is coming at least: winter. Winter is coming, and I need to be gone before then.

I didn't tell you how I found the house, did I?

A mountain house, as much a barn as a place to live, at least three hundred years old, high up in the alpine pasture for the shepherds and

goatherds and cowherds to mind their flocks during summer. A *chalet d'alpage*, they used to call them. This is not a place for the winter; it was never intended to be. Even now, it's someone's rough weekend place, at best. In the winter, the snow will come to the lip of the roof. Or higher. Even with no snow, the closest I can get the car is a fifteen-minute walk away. After my trips to town I have to lug everything up a narrow track in my rucksack.

Water comes from a source, an old pipe runs down through the forest above; the only heat from logs in the pot-belly stove and the log burner, with its wooden (yes, really) chimney. The only electricity; from the generator, and I don't run that all the time, because, to be honest, it's always breaking and I'm fed up with fixing it. The toilet is in a lean-to attached to the side of the house, only reached by going outside.

The house sits at the end of a track, on a slight slope, so that the back is tucked against the hill, and the entrance to the cellar is ground level at the front. There're patches of forest and pasture below, and nothing but forest above until the tree line, another three hundred metres up. As I said, it's very, very beautiful.

I couldn't find anything like this at first. Not where I needed it to be. Then I started hanging out in bars (don't worry) in St Jean and Le Praz and Mieussy and places like that, (making another little triangle), asking around, until I met a guy called Étienne who said, yes, he had a place I could rent.

He brought me here, and showed me around the house but I knew I was going to rent it before I had even stepped inside. I looked at him and said, 'Don't you want to know why an English writer wants to rent a house in the middle of nowhere?'

I'd said it in English, and I wondered if he hadn't understood the expression. He looked at me, for a long time, but then a sideways smile crept on to his face and he replied in English too, 'But this isn't the middle of nowhere. This is the centre of the world.' Despite the smile on his face, I knew he meant it. And who can disagree; for now at least, this is the centre of *my* world.

The centre of the world. That's where I am.

And that's how I'm here; you and Étienne and my damn triangles.

The first I drew was the triangle with Geneva at one corner, and Evian at the second, and the *mer de glace* at the third. I went to the *mer de glace*, by the way; the frozen sea that is the glacier crawling down from the slopes of Mont Blanc, a monster moving in ultra slo-mo, so slow only a god could see its motion across time. I felt some connection then, from the old drawings I've studied. Its crazy fields of ice look just the same as they did when Mary visited it in 1816. They stand like solidified waves, abstract sculptures, fantastical, like creatures from myth, turned to ice.

You know the importance of these three places: Geneva, Evian, the glacier; I think we spoke about them before I left. I drew the triangle. Then I drew three more lines, from each point of the triangle to the centre of the opposite side, to find the exact middle of the three-sided country that I have created. You might be amused to know, though I know these things please me more than they please you, that the house where I have been living these last weeks lies, as far as I can tell, no more than four or five hundred metres away from the very centre of this triangle; which seems to be an almost inaccessible slope just before the real peak of the mountain thrusts to its summit.

Therefore I was feeling pretty pleased with myself. I had more or less accidentally placed myself at some kind of epicentre of Mary's world. Or the world of her creations, it might be better to say. And then. . . ?

Nothing. Nothing.

I hate nothing. All writers do. You always say

at these times that it will come back, but how do you know that, when I don't? What makes you so sure? There are enough people who just stopped writing, for whom the source dried up and was never refilled. Why should I think I'm any different?

Nothing is the precise opposite of what we're trying to do. Like the tragic king said, *Nothing will come of nothing.* You can't make something out of nothing, you make it out of something *else*, something that pushes its way into you, whether you want it to or not. Like love. Or a virus. (Take your pick, but that's what writing a book is like, I've told you that often enough too. You cannot write a book without infection. You become infected, and not until you *are* infected will anything worth writing be committed to paper.)

But then, I thought I had given myself something, with my triangle, with Étienne's house on the mountain, I thought I had given myself enough. Yet it seems I have not. Winter is coming and then I will have to be gone. Already there's been a brief icing of snow on the peak. I didn't see it fall; it came secretly in the night, *like a lover.* By noon it was gone, as quickly as it came, but I know this is the warning. I have to hurry.

And yet, I still have nothing for you, nothing at all.

I dreamed of breathing.

Of the sound of breathing, all around me, up close to me, in the dark of the place where I sleep.

When I woke, it was gone, and, in that moment, I knew it was only a dream.

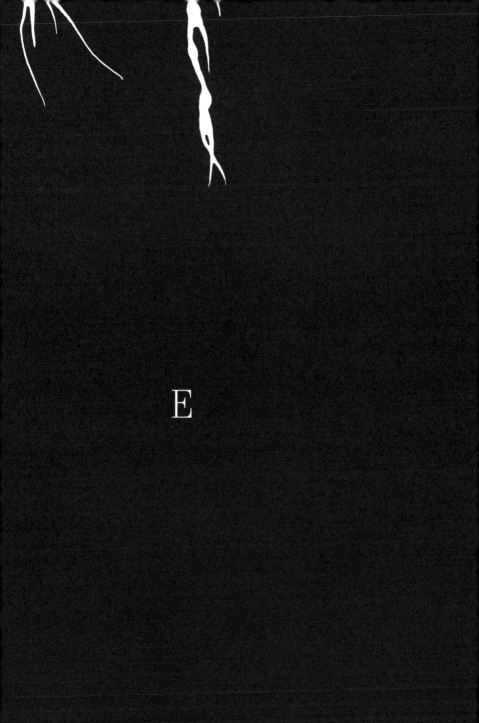

E

Here's something you might like: a short while ago I came out into the tongue of forest below the house and found a dead stump to sit on, shivering as soon as I was away from the sun. Everything was still; that utter stillness that is somehow unnerving, as if Time has stopped. It's not just the stillness; it's the stillness and the trees. I have always loved nature, and forests, but these trees... After a while they start to get to you. I suppose that sounds stupid, but there's just something uncomfortable about the way they stand in their tens of thousands, saying nothing, seeing everything, like I said. I'm sure they add to the sense of being unnerved, so as I sat there, I tried to remind myself that I *like* trees. That they are not something ominous. And yet, there's a vast difference between the gentle oaks and ash trees, and the legion of firs of the Alps. If the light at the foot of an oak is dappled, the light at the floor of a fir forest is practically non-existent.

Nothing seems to live there, nothing moves. A bed of a billion dead pine needles muffles all sound. The ferns do not move. There is the smell of decay, of the spores of fungus. Little else.

As I sat on my stump, the moment became a spell. And it took a living thing; a bird, to flit from the low branch of a pine, to break it. I realised that, along with Time, I had been holding my breath, and then I laughed out loud and shook my head.

It's funny when you spend a long time by yourself. Once or twice I have caught myself speaking my thoughts without realising it; I think I simply needed to hear a voice, even if it was mine. The longest I've been without speaking to anyone, without going to town, is eight days. Eight days without speaking. Doesn't sound very long, does it? Try it. So when I laughed I sort of startled myself, wondering whose laughter it was for a second, before recognising it as mine.

That thin air I mentioned before tricks you in more ways than one: not just the nosebleeds and the dryness of your skin; it makes the sun slice harder, making it feel warmer than it really is. Until you're in the shade and then you know reality. It's. . . cold.

I sat, thumbing through my notebook, looking for something, anything, that could be the key to this whole idea, getting more and more frustrated, colder and colder, till finally I couldn't stand it. I got up and stomped off into a patch of sunlight to warm up again. I stood, fuming for a bit till I realised you cannot be angry in a forest. Did you know? But until then, I was silently cursing you.

That's a lie. I actually told the forest that you were an evil creature for getting me into this, and then I turned and remembered I was in a forest, and, did you know, you can't be angry in a forest, and then I turned again and I thought about soup. And wine, but mostly soup, which drew me back to the house, via the stump to collect my notebook, and it had been totally still all this time, all this time, but as I approached a rare stab of a breeze blew up the valley.

Then this happened: the wind turned the pages of my notebook.

Not all at once. First, one. *Flick.* Then two more. *Flick, flick.* And then another, as if an invisible hand was finding the right place, and just as I leaned over to pick it up, my own hand hesitated as I saw the page on which a solitary line was written – a note to myself:

You despise that book. Destroy it.

That's all, but it's all I need. I know it. It'll be enough. I've started with less. So I hereby declare that I am infected! I'm writing to let you know you'll get your story after all (and then I can leave here before the snows come) but it won't have been me that will have brought it to you – it will have been the wind.

I'll start tomorrow; now I have to have my soup. If the work goes as I hope, I'll have a first draft in a couple of weeks, three at most; you know I work fast once I get going. The really funny thing is I don't even recall writing that line in my notebook. But then, I'm having trouble remembering what I did yesterday, so let's take what we're given, shall we?

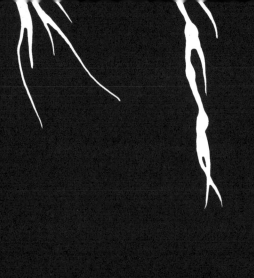

T

There is always the question of where to start. In this instance I can do no better than to say that it started, of course, with *that book*.

I do indeed despise that book. I always have, though I can see that my feelings have ripened over the years. I used to merely dislike it; now I loathe it. It repels me. I know that sounds over the top, but it's true. It repels me in more ways than I can say. I have thrown very few books across the room in my lifetime, one or two only; from anger, frustration. A book is tiresome? You merely set it down. It takes something special to make you hurl a book from your grip: a furiously disappointing ending, for example, one in which you know the author couldn't be bothered to work hard enough to give you something original, something worthwhile.

I look at the copy I own of Mary's abomination and I see it; well-worn, not from loving re-reading, but from the impact of repeated landings on floors and against walls.

I would burn it, but I can't. There's the intellectual's taboo about burning books. We don't do it. We don't.

Where first they burn books, they will in the end burn people too.

Who said that? I have no Internet connection up here; my phone, which I rarely bother to turn on now, shows a single bar of reception, which does precisely nothing. I can't look anything up. Living in this way makes me realise how easy it is to be distracted by the less important points of a story. How often you turn to the world when you should be turning inwards. At first, it annoyed me; now I understand that it is making me focus on what I should focus on – the book, and the infection.

It's been years since I have written in this way. I need some of these details, but they can wait, that's OK – there's a time for research, and there's a time for writing. So as I think of them, I'm writing a list of the things I have to look up next time I'm in town and can get a proper signal on my phone.

Mount Tambora (both heights)
'Beati gli occhi che lo vider vivo' – check
    original source
Neurotoxic effects of butane gas exposure
Exorcism of ice?? Exorcism?!

And now I have written;

Where first they burn books, they will in
the end burn people too.

I have an idea it was a German who said it. A writer, I think. Writers care about books, by and large. Goethe, maybe? No. Not Mann, I'd know if it were Thomas Mann. Heine perhaps. Yes, it's Heinrich Heine. That would be a whole century before the Nazi burnings. Something I do know; that people burn books, and that they ban books is, in a way, a good sign. It's a good sign because it means books have power. When people burn books, it's because they're afraid of what's inside them, and there's the thing: *to be afraid of the contents of a book means that they have power.*

(To be afraid of the contents of a book...)

Orwell's vision of our terrible future was that world – the world in which books are banned or burned. Yet it is not the most terrifying world I can think of. I think instead of Huxley – (did I ever tell you I'm meant to be related to Aldous Huxley? That's the family legend and it's fine by me) – I think of his *Brave New World*. His vision was the more terrible, especially now because it appears to be rapidly coming true, whereas the world of *1984* did not. What is Huxley's horrific vision? It is a world where there is no need for books to be banned, because no one can be bothered to read one.

So, where first they burn books, later they burn people. We have seen that to be true and books themselves are how we can make sure we remember that.

But that's not why I haven't burned this particular book. I haven't burned it because, first, I would only be destroying *my copy*. The Book itself would remain untouched by my puny funeral pyre. Its 'bookness', its existence as a story, is independent of any single copy. Just like a gene in the gene pool. (Remember that email I had from a reader about my last novel? *I want you to go around the world and burn every copy so that no one else has to go through what I did.* I still haven't replied to that one. I surprise you, I know. Yet she had the right idea – you would have to destroy every single copy. But, even if you did, you would still fail as long as one person lived who had read it. Which is why book burners are always doomed to fail.)

So that's, second, why I can't burn it – since

the book is as immortal as any work of human hand can possibly be now, there is nothing I can do. The only thing I can do anything about is my response to it, and if I were to burn it, I would only be admitting that it's under my skin.

And yet, dammit, you guessed this pages ago: it is, isn't it?

A third thought: I haven't always been obsessed with it, far from it. There are books I like much better, books I have read more times, books I have been obsessed with. Long years of my life have turned over, one to the next, without my so much as thinking about Mary Shelley's awful tract, never mind picking it up. Yet there it sits now, on the boards in the centre of the room where I threw it in exasperation two hours ago. It's why I'm here. And it's why I am slowly destroying my reason, no doubt.

Since the book landed on the floor, complaining with a slight rustling of bent pages, I have made myself something to eat, which is no easy trick. I settled for bread and cheese, and soup (again), heated on the ancient gas ring. There is no kitchen here, not really. It's pushing it to call this house a house at all. An alpine chalet, barely touched in who-knows-how-long, few signs of modern things. More like a byre to camp in than a place to live, though someone did, and quite recently, Étienne told me. Of course someone did, I can see the evidence of it.

Such as. . . such as the gas ring on the worktop in the corner that passes for the kitchen. The burner is old and cranky, and is fed by a large bottle of butane gas through a rubber tube that looks as if it might be perishing. I'm not sure the valve is properly attached either, for that matter. Every time I light it I half-expect to be blown sky-high, and to hell with it, that would be a way to go, blown to bits in a remote mountain house, and all because of a book. At least I'd take the blasted thing with me, well, that one copy I own, and that, as I have said, would be an utterly meaningless victory. And yet can you imagine how it would look? The chalet erupting in a fireball of timeworn wood; tin sheets from the roof hurled into the black sky, spinning; the welling, roiling flames; sparks in the dark and the high heaven of stars above as the screen on which would be projected a scene that no one would see.

Assuming the gas supply does not blow me into the dead night sky. . .

I live most of the time in the single sensitive room that forms the top floor of the house – it has a vaulted ceiling of massive wooden beams. Along one side of this space is a shelf, a mezzanine, with a staircase leading up to it that's so steep it's more like a ladder. In the corner, overlooking the valley is the space for cooking; in the corner diagonally opposite is a walk-in cupboard built out from the walls, but I can't get the door open, and my clothes spill over the back of a chair I took upstairs for the purpose.

I have my desk; a crotchety table I stuck by the second window facing the valley, and between there and the 'kitchen' the wooden chimney shoves its way to the roof, twenty feet up. I love the defeated air of the leather armchair that sits before the fire, and next to it a lamp screwed into the centre-post of the house, which gives just enough light to read by, happily. Until you throw the book across the floor, that is...

I opened a tin, heated my soup. I may have opened a bottle of red. I cut the bread I bought this morning and a hunk (what a horrible word, why don't I change it?) of hard cheese and all the time the book lay on the floor, pulsing evil energies at me. I paced past it, pretending not to notice, let it lie there and tried not to go out of my way to avoid it when I took my food to the table, and who am I fooling, of course I would lose that one, for avoid it, or not, it's like an ex-lover you're trying not to think about – either way she or he is there, and he or she wins. All I could do, as I grumpily chewed, was leave it on the floor. I'll leave it there for the night, and only tomorrow when I have to start working on it, will I pick the bloody thing up and treat it with any kind of respect.

Now, I'll give it none, for it deserves none.

It can go to hell. And burn.

T

The generator fails. Again.

Just as I need light to work by.

I stump my feet into boots and out into the night I go, torch in hand. It feebles its way through the darkness; showing me how much I can't see of the nocturnal cold. I come down the slope beside the house. Something always bothers me about the side of the house, but I can't grasp what. It's too dark to think about it now anyway, and maybe it's not the side of the house that's got me puzzled, but something else.

I tread cautiously, picking my way with the torch beam.

Turning the corner, there is a beast. It's a deer; a stag. Its eyes are caught by the torchlight, just as we are both caught by the moment. It stands, planted in the universe in a way I will never be; its eyes glow in the light I'm shining on its face, and then it is gone, with a brushstroke it disappears, arching away into the night, up into the forest above the house. It's left on my mind like a sun print – I see its antlers, such a heavy crown to carry, but one that says: *if I can wear this burden, I have no fear of you.* I see the slight startling on its face as I round the corner of the house. I see its haunches as it slips back into the blackness.

Why didn't it hear me? I must have made enough commotion pulling myself through the heavy old door, scuttling down the slope. Who knows? It's gone.

I turn and with my shoulder shove open another heavy door: ducking through the doorway and into the cellar.

Silence.

It's so silent – the earth floor absorbs sound, the crumbling walls blank me, the darkness is more total than outside, where, if I turned off my torch I would freely see the stars.

I restart the generator, as Étienne showed me. It splutters into life, resentful, I can tell, I can bloody tell, and I come back, and my hand is suddenly wet. Warm.

I put it into the light and see blood and a cut. Quite a lot of blood.

I stare down at the forest below the house. And I turn off the torch. Time goes by. There are shadows. Trunks. The green of the firs is spectral grey in this light, and I turn off the torch, turn off the torch, waiting for the starlight to appear. The cut on my hand. At the back of my mind I vaguely wonder how I did it, and I listen to the trees and there's a slight tapping by my right foot, like a fingertip on a wooden table top. It reminds me of a scene I once wrote in a book but I cannot remember which. My hand stings. The cut zizzes. I must fix that generator. Fix it. Like a gangster fixes a problem with a bullet in the brain, because it is provoking to be beaten by a machine and a fifty-year-old machine at that. I have a book to write. And besides, I want electricity.

I'm in the forest. Trees around me, and I know the tapping was my blood dripping on to the threshold of the cellar, and now hard cut on the forest floor I'm drifting, and ripping my lungs with the ice-air and the thin, thin ice-air knifes me, no, I don't like that, *points* its way into my lungs, ripping with crystals so it's sore, which I can feel, and did you ever think or know or know how we feel our lungs? Our guts? Our blood pump? The frozen wave of fear when you do something bad and, what else is there to say but, the beating of the heart? A beating heart. A beating heart. Say it in time to your beating heart and the forest is the first to witness me, as the generator rumbles in its cave and I know I am struck with the sudden foreshadowing knowledge that I am not going to write this book.

I stumble up.

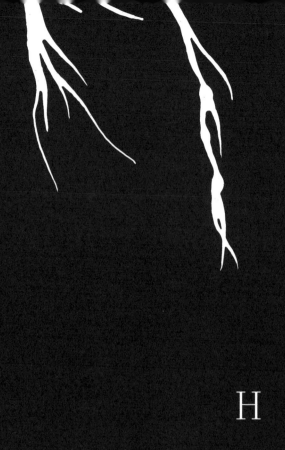

H

I dream of breathing again. All around me. All around me. Close up and so close that it's part of me and I wake, my eyes wide to the cool dark air.

There's still nothing.

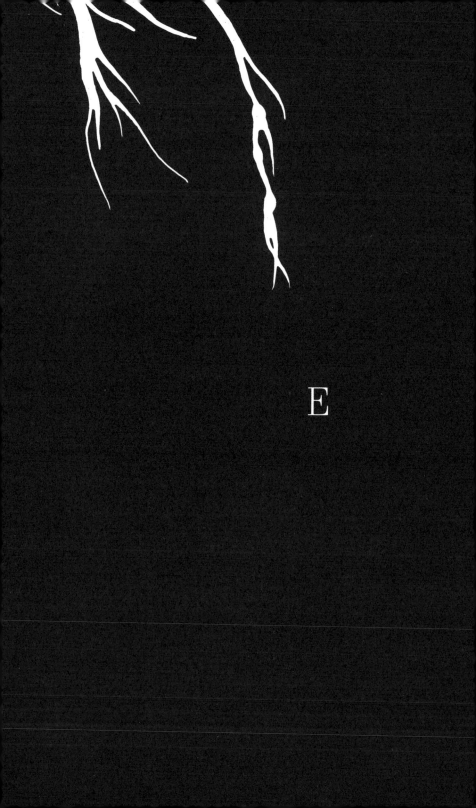

E

It's my daily mantra.

I am, I am. I will, I will.

Down I come from the cramped sleeping area (I am still not tempted to call it a bedroom), which overlooks the space where I cook, wash up, wash, pace and ponder. And don't write.

I set a pan on the burner to make hot water for tea and wonder if I can smell gas again. No. No? I scoop the book from the armchair and take it over to the tiny old table I am using as my desk. My hand throbs.

I stare at it, the book, I mean, as so often, and every time I do I feel some kind of remorse for the fact that I hate it, when everyone else in the world seems to love it, and at the same moment I notice the dozens of folded-down corners where I have marked the passages that irk me and then I only have to open it at any given place and my disgust returns!

Things that offend a sensitive reader's idea of elegance.

Here, let me enumerate.

Exhibit A: *The coincidences.*

The overly convenient chance occurrences that arise again, and again, and again: a symptom of a writer too lazy or stupid to think of ways around such clumsy plot devices.

For example: Victor is a student, away in Ingolstadt, Germany, when he creates his creature. The creature awakes after long toil on Victor's part (sadly we are shown almost nothing of that toil) and Victor, appalled by what he's done, staggers off to wander aimlessly around the city. And after hours of this heedless traipsing and hand-wringing, who is the very first person that Victor encounters? None other than his best friend, Henry Clerval, literally that moment stepping off the coach from Switzerland.

Another. When the creature arrives in Geneva, attempting to track down his creator in his hometown, who is the very first person he comes across? None other than Victor's little brother William, who will shortly become the initial victim of the monster's murderous rage.

Another. When Victor himself later arrives in Geneva, who is the first being he encounters? The creature, of course.

In chapter twenty-one, Victor, wrongly accused of Henry's murder, declares:

> *I could not help being struck by the strange coincidences that had taken place.*

And in a similar way, I could not help throwing the book across the room.

These coincidences are offences against creativity. There are more scattered throughout the book, many more. It would have taken very little effort to have arranged matters so these things fell out as the necessary order of events.

Perhaps such a writer doesn't care about the

coincidences. Perhaps they think the reader doesn't care about them. Both are unforgivable.

Coincidences are one thing. There are more terrible crimes that the book commits. Throughout, there are the bubblings-up of snobbery. And even of its more sinister cousin: racism.

So:

Exhibit B: *Fair is better than dark.*

Everyone recalls how the young Victor is given a 'pretty little present' by his doting mother. That present is, in fact, a human being: Elizabeth, who becomes his adopted sister, his 'more than sister', and later, for one night only, his wife.

Let's not pause to consider the way that Elizabeth is made into an object before she's even walked on to the page properly.

Let's pass over the pseudo-incestuous nature of the relationship between her and Victor.

Instead, let's recall where Elizabeth came from: Victor's parents, while travelling in the lakes of northern Italy, notice the plight of the region's poor. One day, the five-year-old Victor and his mother pay a visit to a cottage, where Victor says, they;

> *found a peasant and his wife, hard-working, bent down by care and labour, distributing a scanty meal to five hungry babes. Among these was one which attracted my mother far above all the rest. She appeared of a different stock. The four others were dark-eyed, hardy little vagrants; this child was thin and fair.*

Learning that this girl is from a good family, a noble one though fallen on hard times, Victor's mother rescues this *celestial*, golden-haired angel from the *hardy little vagrants*, and brings her to live as their own daughter. And good riddance to the dark-eyed peasants, and the hunger of the other four children.

'A good family'. A good family. The phrase, versions of it, and notions connected to it, occur again and again.

But is this Victor speaking? Is it his character's voice? Or is that Mary, the author, speaking?

Mary made Victor, of course, but that does not mean that a character is the writer who wrote him. Of course not. It's more complex than that. (Though people frequently make this mistake when they shout abuse in the street at the actor who always plays villains...)

Whose snobbery is it? Is it Victor's? Mary put the words in his mouth (and of his family), perhaps she was trying to make a point about him – he's detached, a snob, arrogant, and so on. But we are expressly told otherwise by another character.

The book is actually not one story, but four: a story within a story within a story within a story. This structure upsets me too – three would have been good, four feels overdone.

So, Exhibit C: *Clumsy structures.*

To be precise, the book is a series of nested eggs; a Russian doll of a novel:

It opens with:

1) *the polar explorer, Walton, who, while venturing towards the northern polar regions, chances across Victor, who;*
2) *recounts his tale of how he created and then rejected his creature, who then appears through Victor's own account in the narrative to relay;*
3) *his account of how he was made, how he became shunned and how he learned to speak and to read by listening through the wall of the hut of a poverty-stricken family, and is therefore conveniently able to relate;*
4) *the innermost story of the book! Which is the utterly boring and thematically irrelevant (unless the theme of the*

novel really is snobbery) account of some preposterous love affair which brought said noble family to live in said tumble-down cottage in the mountains not far from Ingolstadt.

(This innermost tale is no stranger to bigotry and insipid hatred: we're introduced to 'The Turk', who at last seems to be about to buck the trend that the swarthy are evil while the fair are good, until he turns out to be a devious and manipulative fiend. The fact he's referred to as The Turk, and not given a name, should have been a warning. There's more to be said later about not giving names to things. . .)

To return to the book: in the letters, which open and close it, we learn through the voice of Walton, the polar explorer, that there never was a more inspiring man than Victor, that he is wise and good and eloquent and passionate and and and tragic (of course) but above all, *noble*.

Thus this is Mary's pronouncement upon Victor too. It would be stretching the point to believe that we're meant to think that Walton is deluded in his view of his new friend. That we are meant to read, cynically, between the lines and deduce that they are all as bad as each other. There's so much else that is clumsy and nothing that is sufficiently refined about the book to suggest Mary had anything subtler in mind.

And yet, that is the point: they *are* all as bad as each other, because Mary's own snobbery runs through the book – a strand of its DNA, its genetic code. (If you doubt that, read her travel journals.)

But.

Now I have to stop. It's getting late. Later than I thought. I see we're in the deepest part of the night and I should be sleeping, not whining about this book. Besides which, I can feel something else coming out of me, something I dislike very much to mention. Though I will. I will. I must, if I am to be honest about this business. It's this; there are things I respect about the book. Quite a few, in fact, and I will get to them all, but for now, consider this: it was written by a nineteen-year-old girl, at a time when women were not exactly welcomed as writers, to put it extremely euphemistically. That's remarkable. And I do value that much about it. Furthermore, it achieved lasting fame. That is also a truly remarkable thing for any book to achieve. I've always said that no matter how bad a book; if it is successful then it is fulfilling some function, it has some strong points, there must be *something* good about it, or it would have been consigned to oblivion. It would have been made extinct by the process of natural selection that stories are vulnerable to, every bit as much as animal species.

And now, I hear something – the thing that you probably suspect is the dark in me.

Envy. How can a book this bad have been so successful? Well, there's nothing new about that. Yet what do I think? Can I really step away from my feelings about it as a writer? Detached? Or am I as big a snob as Mary, driven by my envy of its power? I don't know the answer... and then, there's another matter, darker still. And I draw the line under that.

This is not the time to think about such things. I will sleep. And tomorrow, I'll write about the thing I love the most about *Frankenstein*, the novel.

How it came to be.

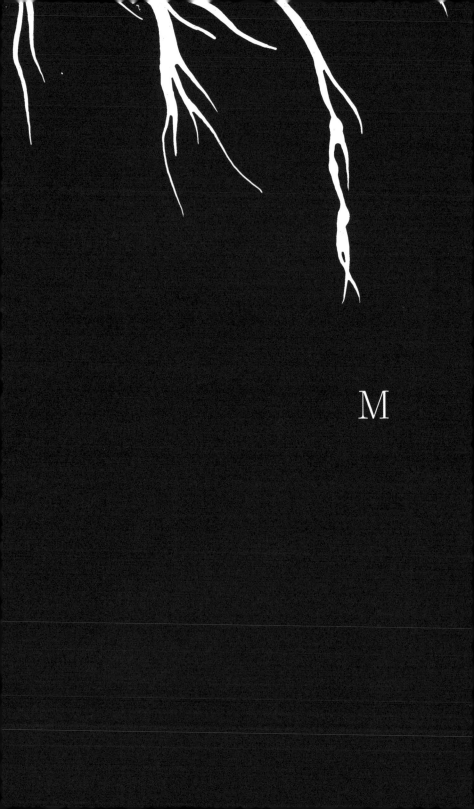

M

You join me at a bad moment. For the night has other ideas.

It's so clear, so true, *so obvious* that the night deals with us differently from the day, that we barely say it. What could be more stupid to point out? But then, that's a daytime voice speaking – it's easy to be clear-minded and rational when the sun is shining.

Try thinking the same thing by darkness and see how different it feels.

Try saying:

There's nothing under the bed,

there's nothing under the bed,

I am sure that there is nothing under the bed,

in the daytime.

Nothing troubling about that.

But say it again when the sun is on the other side of the world, as your candle gutters and wanes, as the shutters gently shift in the wind; then remember that there is barely any wind up here. Listen to the silence that has settled in.

Try it. Hear it. Believe yourself to be in a dark house on a dark mountain in the dark centre of a mountainous triangle, graven on the ground not with stones, or paint, or anything physical, but with the emotions of the dead.

It is dark, it is dark; you cannot see, and that darkness of your eyes is swathed in silence. Is that a noise, or not? The generator stopped again. Did I restart it, or not? Sometimes I can hear it thrumming in the cellar which is far, far down below me, but connected through the ancient bones of the house – its skeleton of massy wooden beams upon which the whole house rests its weight – so sound is transmitted a long way.

Thrum, thrum.

No. No thrum. I left it to sulk. Didn't I? Now it's the middle of the blackness and it's hard to recall, hard to be sure about anything. And yet, I can hear a noise, I can.

It sounds like. . .

…like breathing. Close up. Next to me. Around me. Somewhere, the sound of breathing.

I did leave the generator running. That's it. It's the huff and sigh of the motor as it goes about its ignorant business of making electricity from the multi-million-year-dead mineral remains of microscopic creatures that once crawled across the ocean floor. An ocean floor that is now thrust five thousand feet into the air, and which, covered in interminable fir trees, surrounds me.

Then I remember. I didn't restart the generator this time. I did not, and now I know how I know. I didn't want to cut my hand again in the dark, and as I think that, the cut gives a single zinging throb.

I can hear the breathing. Still.

Slow, deep, right close to me somehow.

Then I know what it is! It's me! So I hold my breath.

Yet the breathing continues.

I listen to it, eyes wide, seeing utterly nothing and focusing only on the breathing, the breathing, the breathing, until, with a shudder, I sit up, banging my head on a beam, fumbling for the electric torch, switching it on and swinging it this way and that in the gloom.

Nothing.

And the breathing has stopped.

I do not sleep again. Not this night. I ask myself this: do monsters always stay in the book where they were born? Are they content to live out their lives on paper, and never step foot into the real world? It's very late before the sun creeps over the mountain opposite and shows itself, by which time I have been clinging to the grey dawn for hours, beaten and drawn, beaten and drawn.

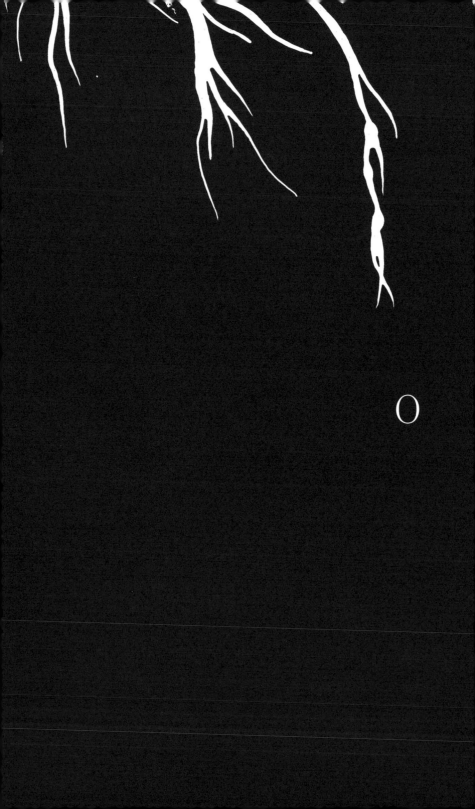

On the other side of the world, people die.

It is 1815. The tenth of April. The Island of Sumbawa.

For several centuries, a monster has lain dormant, miles underground. Now, Mount Tambora's moment has come. For several days previously, warning sounds of detonations have been heard across the Dutch East Indies, as far away as Java, 800 miles distant. The monster is waking up.

Now, at around seven o'clock in the evening on the tenth day of April, 1815, the real eruption arrives. Three columns of fire rise from the peak of the volcano and merge into one. The entire mountain turns into a mass of molten rock. Stones the size of a man's head are ejected into the sky, raining hard on the surrounding landscape.

People flee in horror, but there is nowhere to run. The pyroclastic flow of superheated lava rolls down the mountain and wipes the village of Tambora from the face of the earth. Tsunami spread across the seas, tidal waves devastating communities far, far away.

The mountain blows itself apart. Before the eruption, it stood at 14,100 feet high. By the end, it stands at 9,354 feet, having spewed eleven billion tons of ash and rock into the air, along with poisonous sulphur gases, causing death by lung infection. The ash lies thick on the ground, as deep as 3 feet as far away as 50 miles, destroying crops, killing cattle and livestock, causing starvation and disease. More than seventy thousand people die.

Impenetrable darkness reigns for two days as the ash cloud envelops the proximity of the island. Weeks pass, the ash is swept across the whole world, borne on global winds. 1816 arrives, the weather of the whole planet is affected: in China, the Americas, and on the other side of the world, in Europe, temperatures fall way below average. The ash cloud blocks the light of the sun.

Worldwide climate events wreak havoc; monsoons, crop failures, and fear. In upstate New York, the ground is described as being 'barren like winter'. It's May 1816. By the ninth of June, the ground has frozen solid.

In Europe, famine is inevitable, as crops of potatoes, wheat and oats fail everywhere. Prices rise steeply; riots, looting and arson become commonplace. It is believed that two hundred thousand people die as a result of the famine; with the resulting violence being worst in Switzerland, where a national emergency is declared. People begin to speak about the end of the world. In one town in Belgium, a woman thinks the sounds of soldiers' horns are the last trumpets signifying the end of the world, and throws herself from a rooftop.

The eruption of Mount Tambora remains the largest observed volcanic eruption in recorded history; eclipsing that of Vesuvius, of Santorini, even of Krakatoa.

It is also the reason that a teenage girl called Mary sits down to write one of the most influential tales of horror of all time: *Frankenstein*.

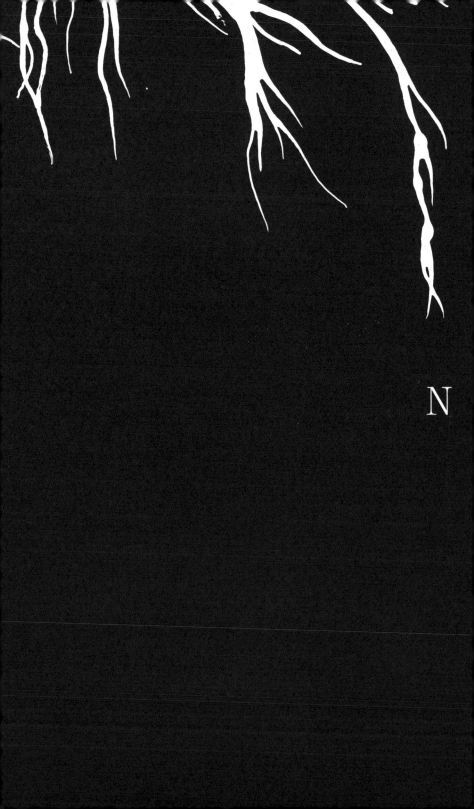

1816: the year without a summer.

Close to the city of Geneva, three young British runaways rent Maison Chapuis, a house in the grounds of the Villa Diodati, which is in turn being rented by a most notorious man – Lord Byron: a great poet, perhaps an even greater villain. Famous for his excesses, and his violent temper. Mad, bad and dangerous to know; that was first said of Byron. Famous above all for his many love affairs, and scandalous liaisons, with men and women, and even boys half his age. The outrage that finally sees him decide to lie low in Switzerland for a while being rumours of incest – an affair with his half-sister, Augusta.

The runaways are the younger poet, Percy Shelley, his lover, Mary Wollstonecraft Godwin, just eighteen years old, and Mary's step-sister, Claire Claremont, a few months younger. Like a woman committing suicide, Claire has come to throw herself at Lord Byron; to rekindle a dalliance of which he has become bored. Mary and Percy have come to escape problems at home; debt and dishonour; having first fled (again with Claire) to Europe two years before, when the girls were just sixteen. Scandal follows them still: Percy remains married to his first wife, Harriet, whom, along with his child, he abandoned, to pursue his affair with Mary,

Completing the party of five is Byron's doctor, and sort-of-friend, John Polidori; a quack by Byron's own admission, but a tolerable drinking companion; an ear for his woes, a salve to his ego.

The party intended to roam the hills outside the city, and sail on the lake, but thanks to a volcano on the other side of the world, the weather lets them down. It is cold. It rains incessantly. They are trapped inside, day after day in an endless twilit debauchery of wine, opium and... more.

They talk, hour after hour, they brood and pace, they throw out wild ideas and discuss the edges of humanity. They read. They read ghost stories; German ghost stories translated into French.

Finally, one night, Lord Byron declares they should each write a ghost story of their own. At first they all agree, yet Percy Shelley and Byron himself seem to tire quickly of the game – they are poets, and prose does not suit them. Claire is not a writer; she does not try. Polidori is not a writer either, but he does; producing a scrap of a story that he would later expand as *The Vampyre*, the first long prose story about the undead creature of horror. And inspired by his employer, Lord Byron.

And then there's Mary, who does not write to begin with, cannot arrive at an idea for days and days, until finally, in some sort of '*waking dream*', she sees a scene of a '*pale student of unhallowed arts kneeling beside the thing he had put together*'.

So, a monster is born.

It's a wonderful story. Not the novel, but how it came to be. Though there's more to it, of course. Things that are odd, things behind the writing of the book that scare me more than any word that Mary would come to write.

Later. There's time for that later. I have to stop now. My hand is throbbing, quite badly; writing seems to make it worse. What a time to cut it, when I need to work, and I still don't really know how. For some reason my head is throbbing too, a headache that's been coming and going for days.

It's long after dark. The chalet is asking to settle down for the night, and I am running out of logs for the stove and the fire; tomorrow I will have to spend some hours bringing more inside.

Cold colonises the wooden walls of the house; the night lifts up. Silence spreads as I put down my pen, my scribbling done. With the scratching of the nib gone, it occurs to me that I ought to be able to hear that breathing. That breathing. Ought? What do I mean by 'ought'?

I listen, I strain, talking myself down from fear and imagination's riots, but there's nothing, and I tell myself I'm tired, and leaving my dog-eared copy of *Frankenstein* on the desk, make my way up to bed.

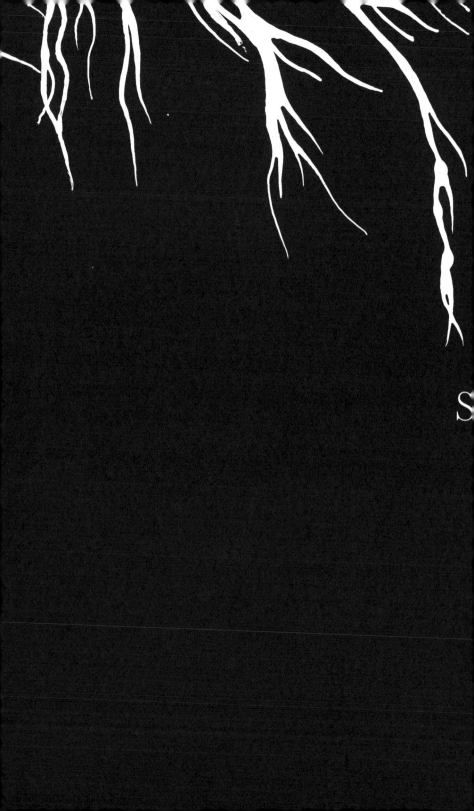

Horror.

It's how I've made my living for almost thirty years. And it's become harder; stories used to flow from my mind like water from the source outside; endless, pure, fresh, free.

Now, making a book is like pulling a root from the ground. It does not want to come. Part of it, I know, is that I have come to detest what I do: I scare people, and if I disturb them sufficiently, I make money. That's what it comes down to, and it's sick. The world is full of horror enough, isn't it? I know we had this conversation six months ago. And I told you I would write nothing more about darkness; that I would write nothing more at all unless it spoke of beauty and light. Yet here I am, pulling roots from the ground, pulling roots from the ground. The world is full of horror enough, and I come face to face with the facts. The fact that people do not seem that interested in mundane descriptions of beauty, or even in beautiful descriptions of the mundane. That they care not for how a thing like a story arrives in front of them, only that they be *gripped* by it. Horrified. And then, the fact that people seem to want to be upset, disturbed, troubled by unreal stories of horror only makes me feel... What?

The only word I can come up with is this; empty.

I feel empty. I feel done.

I woke this morning, scooping the book – the book, the damn book – from the floor where I left it last night, on yes, the floor, and returned dutifully to my desk.

I stare at what I have written; stare, without blinking it seems, staring my writing in the face, staring it down. But I blink first. I stand, so fast I send my chair skidding on to its back behind me, and I flee.

Two days pass. I get no work done. I don't make notes, I don't even try.

Oh.

Yesterday I walked down the track to the car, drove to town, a half an hour of hairpin bends. I am not unaware of the change that comes over me when I leave the mountain, but yesterday it seemed even more pronounced than usual. Something is different on the mountain. Or maybe it's me that's different. How can you decide these things?

Town was normal, so normal, I forgot what I'm doing and why I'm here. My hand throbbed but my head felt better. Clearer. I bought food. I drank a cup of coffee in *Le Central*, nodding at the locals drinking Pastis at eleven in the morning, people whose faces I have seen in this bar or that, and come to know, and like.

Across the street, I saw Étienne. He didn't see me. I sat like a stone, not knowing how to move, not knowing how to leave; finding that the only thing to be done was to stare at my coffee. And then I had drunk it, and I had to move after all. The house was waiting for me, and I could not avoid its call any more, or the pull of the book sitting on my desk.

I drive back up the mountain, noting details I haven't seen before: a chalet or two tucked away in the forest on the hairpin bends; a path into the trees that soon disappeared from sight under a bed of golden-brown beech leaves.

As I lock the car, gathering my shopping, I realise something. I realise that I finally know what has been bothering me about the house, about the side of the house. My mind must have decided to wake up and become alert, and I suddenly have the feeling that I have been dreaming. For a long, long time. Perhaps even for years (and I know since when, if that is the case. . .).

The house.

You enter the living floor at the back of the house – the side highest up. The entrance to the cellar is on the opposite side, facing the valley. Every time I make the journey to the cellar to restart the generator, something bothers me, and now I know what it is. The journey is too far. Too *steep*.

As I get to the end of the track to the house, I dump my bags by the door, without even going inside. Setting off down and around the side of the house once more, heading to the cellar, I judge heights and distances, and then, as I reach the side of the house that faces to the valley, I see them. Windows. Two, shuttered tight. Above them I see the two windows I am familiar with; those by my writing desk and the kitchen area. There is an entire floor of the house I didn't even know existed.

My skin crawls. Something that until this moment I had always taken to be a metaphor appears to be real, a feeling so strong I stare at the bare skin of my arm, to see my hair standing on end.

I stare at the closed, shuttered windows; blind eyes, wondering lots of things at once: such as why Étienne did not mention this floor, why he didn't show it to me, why I didn't notice those extra windows from outside, and, above everything, I am wondering what is hidden in there.

I breathe the creeping sense away from me, I head inside; there must be a way to get to this floor, and I simply haven't seen it before, no stairs to get anywhere apart from the ladder to my bed. I stand in the centre of the room, turning round, gazing, puzzling it out, and then I see it. The cupboard, the walk-in cupboard. It's not a cupboard at all. It's the entrance to a staircase. I know this because the door is open and I can make out a handrail leading into a pit of darkness below.

That's not all.

I head for my desk, where I left the torch.

My notebook is open. It's turned to a fresh double page, upon which a line of writing sits.

It's not my writing.
It's ornate, beautiful, old, old, old.
It says;

I know your secret.

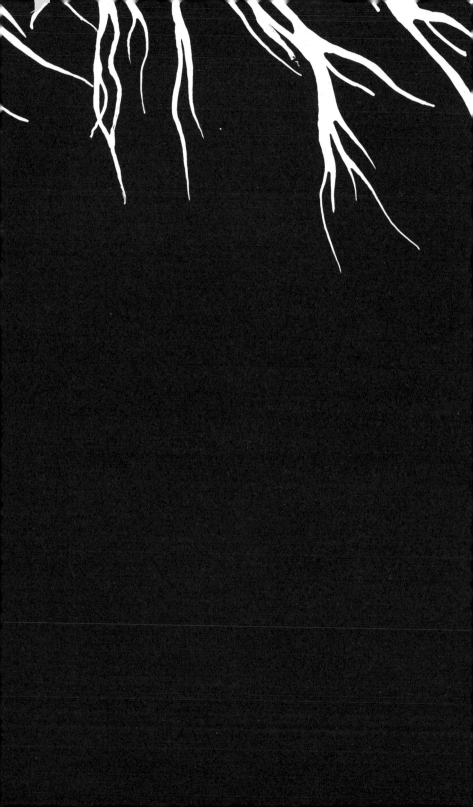

I stood looking—

    No, I stand looking at—

    No.

I stood. I stand.

    I stood, I stand.

    (Why can't I decide which? Why am I having trouble knowing when I am?)

I stand. That's it.

    I stand staring at the notebook, my skin scrawls. I mean, my skin crawls *again*.

    There are two possibilities.

    Someone came into the house, and wrote this. It's possible; I don't lock the door when I go out; Étienne said there was no need. So someone may have come in while I was in town and written in my notebook.

    I stand, staring. I realise that whoever did it has written in English. Not many of the locals speak much English. But some do, and it's not that complicated. As sentences go, I mean. I could manage the same in French: *Je connais ton secret.* My notebook is written in English, of course, so anyone could have seen that and delivered me this message. And then I think, it must be Étienne, but the second I think that, and the second that starts to unnerve me slightly, I know it wasn't him. I saw him in town, not long before I left. I came straight back here – I would have met him somewhere on the road, or on the track, coming back down.

No. It wasn't him. So, there is the door, the door that has always been impassable yet now stands open.

But still I wonder, maybe Étienne is here somewhere; I missed his van somehow and he's here, fetching something from a floor of the house, the hidden floor. He probably just uses it to store stuff.

I take the torch from the desk, and thumb the switch as I step to the top of the stairs. They take three steps down the side of the wall before turning to cling to the returning wall, into the blackness. If he's down there, he's being very quiet.

Maybe he's had an accident!

That thought gets me hurrying.

'Étienne?' I call. 'Étienne! *T'es là?*'

Are you there, Étienne, are you there? I'm repeating in my head, over and over. Are you there, Étienne, are you there? Please be there.

I take each step carefully, slowly. This house is ancient and the torch beam weak, the steps could be rotten and I don't want to break an ankle, all alone in a forgotten house on the mountainside.

'Étienne?'

Nothing.

I reach the bottom of the stairs, and unlike the floor where I have been living; I see I am in a narrow corridor, with doors leading off. The corridor turns a few steps ahead of me, I glimpse another door. The torchlight plays across the floor, across the walls: the wood is old and greyed from its age; a deep brown thick with greying dust, I think, but I wipe my finger across the wall and find no trace of dust on my fingertip.

'Étienne? *Es-tu là? C'est moi!*'

Nothing.

I take a step. I put my hand on a door handle, pressing down on the latch; I hear the lever on the other side flick up. And another noise, from inside?

Did I hear something else from inside?

No. No, you didn't, I tell myself. You didn't. You are to go inside and see that Étienne is not in there.

I push the door open; it's stiff, the hinges creak and the door is so flimsy I feel it might break under my shoulder, but it holds. This must be one of the rooms with the shuttered windows; there is a faint light from outside creeping through cracks. I sweep the torch around me, but the room is empty. Empty, and with a sense of the infinite bridging of time without people in it that really unbalances me, so I withdraw and make my way along the corridor to the next door, on my right this time, the side that tucks into the hill. I push my way in, and the result is as before; the room is empty.

I swing my torch around to be sure and then I see there is something here, after all: an insignificant-looking table; round, its top resting on a central pedestal. It's old. Antique.

I leave the room, and move on: another door on my right, the side against the mountain: I open it too, waving the torch beam. Nothing again.

The corridor turns to the left and I see one more door on each side. I try them both, one after the other. Both doors are harder to open, both rooms are empty.

I walk to the window of the last room; it's the other one with shutters shut tight: I fiddle with some catches – the old glass is thin and cloudy and I'm scared I'll break it, but I manage to open the window, and then cast the shutters open too, without damaging anything, or myself, though my hand is throbbing to remind me of hurting myself, and then I'm looking down over the valley; the same view, more or less, as from the kitchen; just a little lower and closer to the trees.

It's not late, but the sun is already dropping behind the mountain, behind the house; the trees turn from green to grey almost in front of my eyes, and where is Étienne?

I realise that Étienne is not here; that Étienne has not been here, and that there is nothing down here. Not a thing. Except for that table and now in my mind's eye I recall something from looking at it: it's one of those round tables with a flat drum for a top, the sort that has a drawer or two, a narrow drawer, concealed in the drum.

I make my way back to that room, the second I looked into, and there is the table. Yes, it has a drawer. Since it is the only thing here I suppose it is here for a reason, that it has been left for me, and though that makes no sense, I tug the drawer open. Inside, is a key, an iron key, as thick as my forefinger. It has a label tied to it, with a short length of thin grimy string. I pick it up, revolving it between my fingers, and put the torch beam right on it. The label is made from thin white card, aging with spots of foxing, and a reinforced hole. One side is blank, remarkable only for a pattern of the spots forming a perfect triangle. But there is something written on the other side, in old, old handwriting:

Cave.

I stare for a moment or two, trying to work out how you can have a key to a cave, when the thing that is really bothering me surfaces and screams for my attention.

The handwriting on this label, on this old, obviously old, old label, I swear it's the same handwriting that has just appeared in my notebook.

E

I shoved the key back into the drawer, slid it shut, hard. And as I made my way back up the narrow staircase I had the sense, I had the... I could feel things clawing at the back of my legs, feel it as if it was actually happening, but I forced myself not to rush, not to panic, and emerged into the light of the house, and my world.

I closed the door, and leaned against it, making sure it was secure. A chill breeze seemed to have entered the house, so I went over to the door outside, and saw I still hadn't collected the shopping. It was heavy and normal and I put things away in cupboards, normal cupboards that did not lead to staircases to forbidden places, forbidden parts of the...

I tried to think about tins and packets and I focused on each of them... but forbidden is a great word, one with power, I mean, exactly the kind of word I like to use, a word with history, history and power. Everyone knows what *bidden* means; you are encouraged, you are invited to

do something. Or to go somewhere. And that *'for-'* part at the start is a prefix from the old languages of the North, meaning against; it denotes an opposite; just the same as *'un-'*. We are *not* invited. We are *not* allowed. We are forbidden to enter the dark rooms of the mind where—

What? Who said anything about minds?

Put the shopping away, I put the shopping away and the room was getting dark, so I tried the light switch that turns on the little light by the armchair and I cannot say how happy I was when it came on, the generator was running and I sank into the chair to think what to do.

I'm still thinking what to do. But what do I mean? There isn't anything to do. I came home, I put the shopping away, I found the house has an unknown area. No, that's not right. It didn't happen in that order. And I left out a couple of things, but maybe I'm just tired, the air is so mean, I mean thin, up here and I thought I had got used to it but maybe I haven't quite yet.

Do I smell gas? No. Then, I go to my desk, because maybe I imagined the whole thing, then, no, I nodded off in the armchair and now it seems real but it isn't but when I get to the desk there is my notebook still.

I know your secret.

I stare at it. Well, then, someone came in and is trying to play games with me. Maybe someone who knows the house. Not a burglar, because there is my laptop on the floor beside the desk, where I left it.

I shame my hands. I mean, I shove my shameful hands into the pockets of my fleece. There's something solid in the right-hand pocket and before I take it out I know what it is. The key from the drawer of the old round table downstairs in the darkened rooms sits in the palm of my hand, and—

I stare at it – I stared at it, I mean.

(When am i? I mean, when am I? *I*.)

Staring at the key, staring, and I recalled then that I'd slipped it into my pocket, downstairs. That's right.

And I wondered what it was the key to, so I tried a few doors. Not many options. Not the key to the cupboard door, the cupboard that isn't a cupboard, I mean, and then I tried it in the main door to the house, but I already have a copy of that key and it's much larger than this one. Then I remembered what *cave* means in French. Not 'cave' at all; it's a false friend, isn't it? A false friend, it's pronounced 'carve' and it means cellar.

Outside, shivering now that the sun had gone, round to the cellar, remembering that Étienne had never given me a key to the cellar door. It's just stiff and heavy and there's nothing inside to steal but the generator, and good luck with that; the beast weighs a ton, obviously.

But it wasn't the key to the cellar either; I could see before I even tried it that the keyholes were different sizes and shapes. Inside the cave, the generator was humming away to itself, and I smiled, but then, as I turned to leave, it stopped. So I had to curse it, and shove the door open and go inside to fix it again. I hadn't brought the torch but it was light enough outside to half-see what I was doing and I swear I could do it blindfold now, I've done it so many times: re-prime the pump, pull the handle hard, hope. That's all there is to it. My hand throbbed, my cut right hand, but throbbing means healing, doesn't it?

I had no idea about the key. I held it in my fingertips as I came back round and up the slope to the door. The label blank on one side, the writing – *cave* – on the other.

Inside, I collected the torch, marched straight

downstairs again and this time I really did shove the key back into the drawer.

Upstairs, I closed the door behind me, checked it was shut, and went to start thinking about making something to eat. I don't know how long I was doing that, fussing about, taking things out and putting them away again and I fixed on something, putting water on the gas ring to boil and no, the house didn't blow up, but then I thought it was getting really cold, so I went to light a fire. At the armchair. . .

At the armchair, by the fireside, I stopped.

Sitting on the seat was my copy of the book.

And sitting neatly on top of that was the key.

I stared at it, something nagging about it, and as I forced myself to start thinning, I mean thinking, again, I saw what it was. The writing on the label. It had been blank on one side; *cave* written on the other. Now I saw a new word on the label: *piège.*

I stared at it for the longest time, the longest time, glaring at it, willing it not to be here, wishing this were not happening, but it was, and finally I had no choice. I had to see. I flicked it over, expecting to see the word '*cave*' on the other side, but it was blank. And yet, it was clearly the same key, the same label; I even recognised the little pattern of foxing spots from before.

Piège. Not *cave*. I think that I must have read it wrong before. But how could I have? *Cave* is nothing like *piège*.

I backed away, keeping my eyes on it, and turned to the cupboard where I've been keeping a bottle of whisky for just such occasions as this, for just such, such just such occasions as this when I think I might be losing my. . .

. . . for just such occasions when I need to get extremely drunk.

So I did.

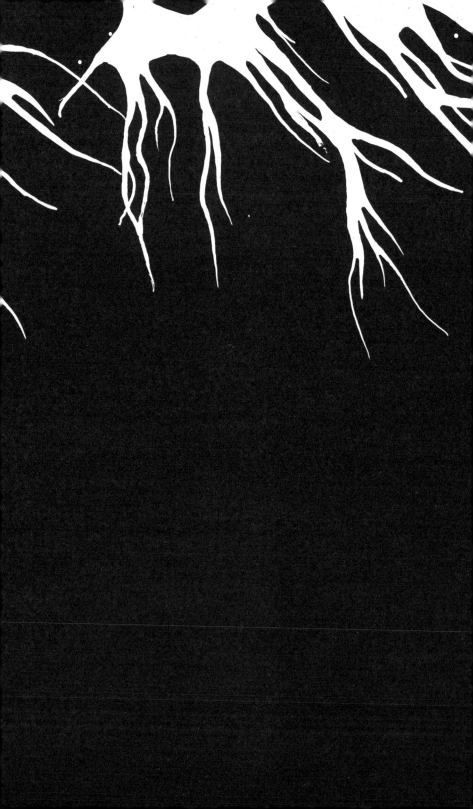

R

Shoved. Then. Thoughts. Desk. Map. Silk dress. Ink. Forced. Grey. Time. Down. Forest. Creature. Sun. Wrenched. Hum. Door. Snow. Steps. Glacier. Gas. Hysteria. Burned books. Savage. Love. Birth. Empty. Repetition. Easy. Neglected. Table. Cut. Key. Key. Pioneer. Electricity. Charnel-house, bone-yard. Still-born. Colour. Lake. Hut. Door. Door. After. Elicit. Open. Hand. Neurotoxin. Healing. Breathing. Breathing, hear breathing. Here. Breathing. Close. Forest door. Key writing. Prowling. Home sorrowful and away. Fortune, fate, frightful. Pronouncement. Dress. Grey dress, dark grey dress. Ink on crinoline, band of hair, brush of fabric on boards. Cold, cold. Stab. Lungs pointing. Air, rent of floor forest door. Grimly. Quietly. Hidden.

And this by daylight.

And this by my mind's tugging, forced thought to pull up, pushing against the trap of the drink. Failing, falling, then rousing and I start to surface. But fall again. Time. More time. Rousing. Dying.

Drowning. Withdrawn. Published. Created and sold, created and abandoned. Dead after thirty-three years. Dead after seven days. Dead two months early. Horror; hysteria. Gas. A mind with its meaning and the falling of leaves on the forest floor. Hum. The Humming. Gas. Silence. *Piège*. Door. Key. Footsteps and snow. Footsteps and snow. And I make another. . .

I make another effort, before the daylight goes.

And when am I? I mean where, of course. Where. Where?

It's cold. I'm cold, which is more. Which is more.

I sit up and still my eyes are shut.

Outside.

Outside, cold. Hard underneath. I open my eyes, I open my eyes and I mean I really have to make my eyes open. Moon. Clouds. Moon behind clouds, halo of brown-light, silver-faced moon. I retch.

Doorstep, under porch.

Late.

I don't remem—

Yes, I do. Some of it.

With a stab; the key.

And *piège*. What does *piège* mean? What does it mean?

I cannot remember. Maybe I never knew, French was never my strong—

Wait.

The key moved.

The book moved.

Or do I mean: the book, moved?

Small things, small things. You must look out for the small— Did it move itself or did someone move it. . . ? Of course it didn't move itself. People move things. People move commas. Writers move commas, and commas do not move themselves, because things do not move themselves. People move things.

I sit up straighter, my head bangs from the drink.

I shudder, try standing.

Throbbing.

I need coffee. Maybe even water. I have some tablets. Somewhere I have some pills.

I do stand and the world is still spinning. Glance at sky. Trees, trees, trees. But sunlight has gone. It's late then. I was away for some time, some deal of time.

I stagger and shoulder the door open, back into the house. Back into the house. Have to make, to boil some water. Coffee, and the house will be cold and I will have to light a fire or I will—

No. I will not have to light a fire. A fire is already lit. The house is warm. The firelight flickers on the white lace hem of a grey silk dress, a dark grey silk dress. I imagine touching the silk and it would feel like cobwebs, and yes, there is someone in the armchair. The book sits by her hand. There is the smell of gas.

Hearing me come in, she stands. She stands.
She does not smile.

'I was never drunk,' she says. 'Not once.'

S

She's in middle-age, and it takes me a moment to decide that she is who I think she is. We are so used to thinking of her... thinking of her as young, as that young girl, running away from home at sixteen, writing her book at eighteen and nineteen... but what of her after that?

What of her after that is what I see before me.

She must be around fifty, I judge (and didn't she die at fifty-three?).

She fixes me with an unnerving gaze, and I am duly unnerved. I open my mouth. Shut it again. Lift a hand, let it drop. She stands by the armchair, and in her hand is my copy of the book. But the book is hers, not mine.

When we read a book, though, we call it *ours*, don't we, and I have always said that's because readers make a book their own through reading it. They do half the work, with their own imaginations, fleshing things out, painting each character and place and event in more detail than we have actually set down on paper, and we writers merely set the readers on their way. So it is my book too. Her book. My copy of her book. And that copy is in my mind as much as it is in her hands; it's in my damn mind forever.

Her mouth moves, and she speaks. She lives.

'What has brought you here?'

I stare at the book in her hands. She doesn't look at it, or make reference to it. Yet we both know it's there.

She is standing, I am standing. Nothing passes. Finally I know I have to give some kind of answer.

'Triangulation,' I say. 'I suppose.'

She considers this. I see the word 'triangulation' whisper across her lips, thoughtfully; underneath I already see that famously bold spirit.

'That,' she states, 'is an answer with no small degree of perfection.'

She seems satisfied. But her brown eyes stay fixed and do not smile, her mouth is narrowed.

From where I stand I feel her grey cobweb silk under my fingertips and there's that smell of something again: something mineral, something dead.

I want to ask her a question. Of all the things I could say, I want to ask her a foolish question.

'There is a matter on your mind.'

I wonder if it was that obvious or whether she knows what I am thinking. My god, I hope she doesn't know what I'm thinking. As I'm wondering whether that is true she says, 'Is this you?'

Her book is gone. I must have been mistaken. For now her book is gone and she's holding my notebook in one hand and with a fingertip of the other she's tapping my name where I always scrawl it in capitals across the cover.

My throat constricts, and I find I cannot speak.

I nod a yes, and she says, 'We have the same initials. Amusing.'

I start to smile but the smile dies on my face, with a trembling of the lip, as it is not returned.

'I'd never thought of that,' I say, almost to myself.

She turns back to the armchair, and sets herself down in it.

'What is the thing you wish to ask me? My arm?'

Now I know she must be able to read my mind. There is no other explanation for it. Her arm. It hangs awkwardly. She is using it, but it seems to move somewhat differently. We know it affected her as a girl, but no one knows what happened, whether she was born with a problem of some kind, or if some accident befell her.

'You want to know what afflicts my arm? Are there not more interesting questions you wish to address? Did you tri-an-gu-late for such trivialities?'

She draws the word out. Is she mocking me? She may merely be enjoying the word (I do the same myself sometimes) and all the time I am thrown, truly thrown.

'Very well,' she's saying, 'we have made our

introductions. I have confirmed your identity. And you know who I am, correct?'

I nod.

'Do you do more than nod?'

I just catch myself and drag a question out.

'What, then,' I stammer, 'I mean, what are you – what are you doing here?'

Now her mouth forms a smile, but it's a cool, unkind smile and the pit of my stomach knots.

'May I offer you a chair?' she says, and points at the wooden chair I use at the desk. I fetch it, and know that I am bothered by her offering me a chair. This is my house, at least while I rent it, and it belongs to Étienne the rest of the—

'Good,' she says. 'Excellent. You ought to keep warm, no doubt you are feeling the effects of your libations.'

I follow her eyes to the empty whisky bottle lying on the floor, one beautiful golden drop still left inside. I feel my cheeks redden. I feel a touch nettled too.

'Did you light the fire?' I ask, still asking all the wrong things. When she doesn't answer, I sit the chair a few feet away, facing her, slightly tilted to one side, for looking at her straight on is too much.

'How old are you?' I ask.

'One doesn't ask such questions,' she says. 'In my day. But then I never paid much care to the conventions of my day. I'm fifty-three years of age.'

I wonder if she knows she's dead. But then, she isn't. At fifty-three she was still alive. Just. Anyway, she's sitting in front of me, that's more alive than many people. Then I wonder if she's about to die and whether she knows that moment is—

'What do these signify?' she asks, and then I know I'm sunk.

Her book is in her hands again. Her copy of my book, no, I mean, my copy of her book; the one with all the corners bent down, the corners that mean...

'I mark. . . I mark pages, pages of significance. Significance to me, that is. So I can find them easily when—'

'What do they signify?'

My mouth dries, and my throat constricts again, as if two fingers are pressing on my Adam's apple with insistence.

'I. . . That's to say, I mean. . . I—'

'What do they signify?' she repeats, her voice dropping a note or two and I find that I really don't want to answer.

She stares at me, her gaze penetrating me in ways I do not like. I see her move, she puts down her book, and picks up my notebook again. I don't let anyone look in there, anyone. She leafs through it like a magazine, until she stops, evidently finding what she's looking for.

'"You hate this book",' she says, quoting my words at me, '"Destroy it."'

She lifts her gaze.

'So, what are these turned down corners?'

There is nothing to be done. I know she knows more than I am saying.

'They are passages in the book,' I say quietly, and without looking at her, 'which I find. . . less than. . . convincing.'

She says nothing at first.

Then she simply says one word.

'So.'

I have no idea what that means.

'Would you care to give an example of such moments?'

I would not. I say nothing.

'Let me put it like this; why do you hate my book so much?'

I stare at the floor, at a space between the tips of her silken shoes, which protrude from beneath the hem of her dress.

'Come now, what you intended to say to your reading public, you surely are bold enough to say to me, the target of that approbation?'

I sigh. She has me. This is just how I feel about

the people who so freely declaim a writer's work in public forums; I doubt many of them would be so rude or so clever to say it to the writer's face. *So,* I have to confess she has won the argument, but I still don't want to list a book's perceived faults to the woman who wrote it.

'You were very young—' I venture, but she cuts me off.

'I don't believe you think that has anything to do with it. Do you? No, I thought not. We both know that my first book was my best. And I dare a little immodesty in pointing out the obvious to you: it has become a pinnacle of the literary canon, remaining in print for two hundred years. And wildly influential. Can you say the same about any of your writings? I don't believe you can. Except maybe one that will stand the test of time, and of that one, well...'

She trails off and I do not like her implication.

'Maybe you think,' she goes on, 'that something you pen will achieve the immortality of my masterpiece? Perhaps, yes. Probably, no. So I ask you again: what is it about my book that you have such intense dislike for?'

She's goading me, deliberately. But successfully it seems, because I find I have the nerve to fight back.

I wave a hand in the air.

'It's clumsy. I believe one of your most forgiving biographers said the book is "beset by many faults, weakened by improbable situations".'

'Yes, I remember that account of my life and work. We also share the same initials as that particular biographer; did you not observe that either? What else besides? Perhaps you believe your own work to be above criticism? You only deal it out to others, is that right?'

Very well, I think. You're asking for it.

'Simple weaknesses in the plot; the large number of overly convenient contrivances that could have been easily avoided. Aside from Victor and the creature, your other characters are weak. The style is overblown at some points, at others crushingly banal. And I don't forgive your age, or the era in which you were working – Jane Austen was producing her finest work around then, wasn't she?'

I know I have gone too far now, but I don't seem to be able to stop. I have the floor, I may as well say my piece.

'But fundamentally, I would happily ignore all these faults and imbalances, happily, were it not for one thing. Your book displays snobbery—'

'Yes?'

'Elitism—'

'Really?'

'And racism.'

'Racism? You find it xenophobic? You must remember that it's a work of fiction, and that the words of my characters do not—'

I cut her off this time.

'Don't try to pull that one. Of course I know that, I may be a bad writer but I am a writer.

You're using that defence retrospectively, and one only has to read your private letters and diaries, as we all have, to see your views on the "indolent French", the "slothful Asiatics", and the shabby working classes in general.'

'"As we all have",' she quotes me back. 'Many people have read my private letters?'

The note of paradoxical arrogance underlying this question does not escape me. I chew it over, then spit it out.

'A few people.'

She's silent for a time, staring at the fire. I seem to have won this skirmish, but I have a pressing feeling that I am far from winning the war, not least because I don't know what the war is. I am suddenly aware of the space of the house; the air it occupies and which occupies it, of the hanging weight of it, high up here at five thousand feet, and the empty night rising out of the ground as dusk arrives in the mountains, and down in the gorge, ringing chasms throat roaring water into fathomless depths, unseen by Humankind and all but the bravest of beasts, while I sit and converse with a woman long dead.

Around her neck she wears a bivalve locket, the kind with a picture in each half, or, in this case, as I already know, two locks of hair. It's covered in fine, dark green leather. I have seen it before. I saw it in a museum in Oxford, ages ago. Ages. Yet it sits now around Mary's neck, resting on her chest. I wonder briefly if air is passing into and out of those lungs, then the firelight catches the inscription on the locket, set in brass filigree. I don't need to get closer to read it.

> *Beati gli occhi che lo vider vivo.*
> *Blessed are the eyes that saw him alive.*

Time bends above our heads as the fire licks the soot from the inside of the stove and she thinks her memories and I think mine, and then she tilts her head towards me again.

'You are not going to complete your project,' she states, with such certainty she might have been talking about the coming of the night.

'No?'

'No. For all your... dislike of my book, you are clearly aware that it has reached into you. Furthermore, I notice you do not mention one of the criticisms that is most frequently levelled at it...'

She wants me to ask, and I do.

'Which is?'

'That it was not even my idea in the first place – this hideous tale of a man creating a monster – but was suggested to me by the conversing of my husband, and his... mentor.'

'Lord Byron?'

'Yes, you know who I mean, and you know the episode to which I refer – it was their discussions of galvanism and modern natural philosophy that I listened to. They wondered aloud about the reanimation of the dead. And lo! That was the story I wrote. I wonder why you don't care to list this among your compilation of the faults of my book.'

She fixes me with that gaze. I hold it for a moment.

'But that isn't a fault with the book itself. Everyone takes inspiration from somewhere, don't they?'

'Don't they indeed,' she says. 'Would you care to enlarge upon this subject?'

No, I think. I would not. I keep my mouth shut. She lets it drop.

'Anyway, all this is beside the point. And in some ways, I agree with you. There is one matter, however, that is more important than all of these other matters.'

'Which is?'

I find I have begun to talk more formally, more in the way she's speaking.

'Which is that there is something I need from you.'

Not for the first time I am unable even to find words, never mind the way to say them.

'From the start,' she says. 'From the very outset, my book has been misunderstood. And so it is hardly to be marvelled at that no one understands it now, when from the outset it was misinterpreted. I can no longer allow this to happen. I need the true meaning to be disseminated. And you are the writer who is going to make that happen.'

I lift my head sharply.

'No,' I say. I almost laugh, but there is nothing funny about this situation. 'No. I am not that writer.'

'I'm growing weary,' she says. 'I need to retire. I give you three days to think it through. Ask yourself questions if you like. . . And I might say, it is conceivable, after my having come here. . . that there will be other visitations. I suggest you consider everything that has been said. I should add that. . .'

She falls silent. I wonder if it is true that even

ghosts grow weary, that even ghosts tire. And then I think, my god, of course they must, faced with an eternity of nothingness. Who would not tire? Is she trapped here, in the centre of a triangle of her own devising? Or perhaps I have conjured her, with my magical triangles.

I see she is waiting for me to ask her to continue.

'What?' I mumble. In protest, I get up and pretend that the stove needs more wood. Opening the door, I throw a log to the flames.

'I give you a word of caution. I suggest you beware other visits, especially if that visitor turns out to be my creation.'

I turn towards her, and see that she has disappeared.

Staring at the chair where she was sitting does not make her come back, and she is not the only thing to vanish: the fire is out. Where a moment before the log burner had been roaring, it is dead. I put my hand on the top of it. It's cold.

W

What is it that makes us create? What drives us to carve images in stone, to daub ochre and charcoal on the walls of caves? Why do we put oil on to canvas, blow notes of music into the air, why do we make marks on paper? Some would have you believe it's all a waste of time; some random and essentially meaningless by-product of evolution that expends our energy on frivolous things, unimportant things; things unconnected with the central matters of life: food, clothes, shelter.

These people are wrong.

Almost everyone has an inborn need to create; in most people this is thwarted and forgotten, and the drive is pushed into other activities that are less threatening, less difficult, and less rewarding. In some people, the need to create is transmuted into the need to destroy. Underlying both is the need to understand the world and to interact with it; and creation is a frightening act; one that takes courage, or at the very least naivety, while destruction is both easy, and (maybe) surprisingly, much safer.

To understand the world. To understand what we are doing here when we are dropped on to a spinning rock in space, opening our eyes in wonder at the utter confusion of it all.

Confusion. That's what it is.

You want horror? Isn't that horror enough? We're born into confusion, and there are but two responses to it.

Creation. And destruction.

As soon as Mary left me, I was struck, as if by an invisible blow.

I fell back on to the wooden boards of the chalet and my body smacked them like a hand on a drum. The house reverberated then, echoing in the hidden rooms that lay beneath me, and I wondered if Mary was down there, while at the same time knowing I could not go and find out.

No doubt, in the darkening forest below the house, the stag was at large, its immodest antlers ducking under low boughs while I lay on the floor with my throbbing hand, slowly healing. Away across the mountaintops I could sense the cold lifting of the night; early stars emerging on to the ink-sheet, frost nipping the leaves of the few deciduous trees, leaving bare spindles to await the following spring.

I lay, and time melted deeply into me and then I thought about what Mary had said.

Beware of my creation.

E

I relit the fire. Or should I say, I lit it for the first time that evening, then sat and waited out the long night in the armchair, sitting where Mary had sat, wondering many things, not least the pressing question of whether I am losing my mind. I felt very little, save apprehension about what might come, and how it might unveil itself to me, unveil itself. But nothing came.

Eventually, I slept, and dawn woke me with stiffness in my neck and back and the chilling air of the house without the fire.

I pulled myself from the chair, and went to throw open the door, wanting the cold to wake me up properly. There was an inch of snow on the ground, no more.

Then I pulled myself from my chair while I realised that I was already standing by the door. I shook my head, trying to understand what was happening, and while I did, I watched the snow steadily melt. And then I pulled myself from the chair.

By lunchtime, the snow had gone. The sun bowled over the high lip of the mountains opposite the house and the world began to steam with the evaporation of the damp from wooden surfaces, from the tin roof of the house, from the roof of the woodshed, from the flat stones that lay beside the stone water trough.

Then there came a time of space in which I knew nothing more than that a dead woman had shown herself to me and I knew most profoundly that things were starting, not winding up, as I had thought. I had thought that time was closing and I was in that all too short and lovely spell of creation and now I saw that what I was doing was not writing, not creating, but that I had been co-opted into an act of re-creation.

You want more words? I have none. Why are more necessary? Why? Are people so stupid that they do not see what has been put in front of them in black and white? Or not stupid, but rushed, hurried for time? Too harried to understand the words? And this despite the fact that the words are not only in black and white, but black and white that they can choose to reconsider. It only takes some moments to flick back and re-read, doesn't it? And this is not a gift the moving picture theatre offers you, is it? Nor can you have a singer skip, re-skip and repeat at your whim. So if you have missed something, here, in black and white, then you could enable your god-given right to remind yourself of everything I have said so far; I promise you it is enough.

And you, I give you this, you always taught me to say *less*. You always taught me to draw back where others would waste a dictionary's worth of words, for things that have already been stated, in black and white.

But, here:

I give you this too.

A dead woman came to me, and spoke. She bid me to do her work, where she could not.

And I am not of a mind to obey.

I went to bed, I can't say when, but the sun was sinking and the cold started to draw itself up and around the house and the whole sky became grey, and I sensed bones approaching.

I lay on the bed in the dark, and there was breathing in my ears, right up close, breathing, breathing, and the gentle but persistent pressing of a mighty thumb and finger on my windpipe.

D

Some distance was required. A walk, to put some space between the things pressing in on me: the house, my mind, the house and its secrets, and Mary.

I'd determined to be straight out, but it took me hours to get sorted, for every time I found myself on the doorstep, pulling on my walking boots, I would stand and prepare to leave and then clomp back inside to pick up something I thought I had forgotten. Then I wouldn't know what it was and I would stare at the wood turning grey with age all around me, and the cold fire, and then I would get to the doorstep where I would pull my boots on. Then I would have the feeling that I had forgotten something and I must have pulled my boots on a dozen times but I'm really sure I only did it once.

Finally, with some great effort not to think, I found myself on the path leading up from the house, away from the path down to the car, and town, and towards the high mountain. This meant pushing under the hanging branches of the final strip of forest before the climb really started, feeling the scrape of their needles on my neck here and there.

It was a cooler day, even in the sun, and in the gloom of the forest, cooler still, and I was glad I had brought a fleece to wear. I turned up its collar, pulled my woollen hat further down, trying to focus on nothing but each boot step, and listened to the sound of the dead forest floor giving with each footfall, the rustle of my clothes and the creak of the arms of the trees in the soft breeze. Patches of sun fell through gaps in the branches, and I could see past the trunks to sunlit alpine grass, tall and dying as winter approached.

I could still hear the cascade of water in the gullet of the valley, so soft and dispersed now, just white noise, white noise. I passed beyond the treeline to the open slopes, following a path trod into the ground by centuries of hooves, of goats, of cattle, of the mountain sheep and the occasional foot of Man, where, tilting my head against the high horizon, I made mental trigonometry. It might take an hour. Or maybe two, but I knew it was probably deceptive. Still, there, out of sight, was the peak of my mountain, the very centre of not just my triangular world, but the entire planet itself, and I had not yet visited, despite the weeks I had whiled away in my rotting gorge. I needed space, and I knew the peak of the mountain would offer it in infinite abundance.

The whole face of the heavens was blue, across the compass, just a wisp of white here and there, sidling from behind the peak, but which dissipated as fast as they arrived. I climbed, and inoculated by sunshine, I found ways to forget what had happened, for an hour at least, perhaps more. Yet still the peak was out of sight and as far away, therefore, as when I had set off.

As tired as old ghosts, I found a rock and let myself rest, trying to suck what little oxygen there was from the miserly air, gazing back down on the way I had come: the valley, the forests. There were glimpses of the winding road before it turned out of sight, glimpses of mountain streams before they entered the chasm of the valley, and then I saw a roof of a chalet.

Thinking it had to be mine, I smiled. It looked so innocent in the drifting afternoon, not a place of forbidden matters, but then I realised it was not my house at all. The roof was made of corrugated iron sheets, just like Étienne's place, but while his had been replaced fairly recently and were mostly still steel-grey, this roof was rusting orange-brown across its entire surface. The configuration of the two chimneys was different. It was hemmed in by trees on all sides, unlike Étienne's house. Yet I knew it couldn't be far from where I had been staying these weeks, and I felt very stupid that I hadn't seen it before.

I watched it for a time, as if it would do something, then laughed at myself, because, what would a house do?

It started to get cold, and I twisted round to look at the peak behind me and saw not just a few wisps of cloud but banks of darkness sweeping over from the other side of the mountain. They soon took the sun, and the temperature plunged. A ferocious wind slapped my cheek. I sensed there was something in the clouds, and soon saw ugly grey streaks of diagonals across the mountain. With that, I turned for home.

I wasn't even halfway down the open slopes when the rain hit me, pattering on my shoulders as I hurried. Before I had closed the other half of the distance to the forest, the rain became sleet, and within no more than a minute, thick, heavy, wet snow. I put down my head and though I had my fleece, it was not waterproof, and the chill of snow started to seep into me. As I entered the protecting trees I made out another path, leading around the edge of the forest, and knew it was heading towards the other house whose roof I'd seen. I felt drawn to explore, but equally

I felt pushed away. Besides, I knew it was ill-advised, to say the least, when I was already cold, and while the snow was getting heavier.

Inside the forest it was almost too dark to see now, and though most of the snow was kept from me, here and there a few solitary flakes would drift down in front of me, calm, having been removed from the will of the wind.

By the time I made it home I was shivering badly. Somehow I fingered a fire into life in the log burner, pulled off my sodden clothes and slumped into the armchair with two blankets across me.

I slept, waking fitfully then dozing again, vaguely thinking about triangles and the centre of the world. I thought about being trapped. About ghosts being trapped, about ghosts being tired. I thought about other creatures, other monsters, about stories from the mountains; stories I'd read about tunnels in the mountainsides, about pits deep inside caves, full of treasure, guarded by spirits and demons, and then I remembered how they used to think glaciers themselves were spirits. In brutal winters they would grow, descending from the Alps to destroy barns, houses, even whole villages, unstoppable, though they did indeed try to stop them. They called on bishops to come, and the bishops tried to exorcise the ice. Exorcise the ice, and remove their evil spirits, but in vain, of course.

And then I must have slept into the small of the night, because when I woke; my new visitor stood before me in the wavering half-light.

E

Firelight gives him an eerie glow.

I know. And I try to ignore.

I know who he is, but he seems to want to make sure.

He stands there, waves an arm in front of his body as if drawing a sash in the air with the backward sweep of his wrist.

'Do you know me? Do you know me?'

I nod. How can I not? I have read his description a hundred times, after all: not his physical appearance so very much; but his behaviour, his actions. The wildness in his eyes, the air of intellect and fierce emotion; the still undimmed belief in goodness, hidden far below a surface of tragic pain. My god! I half-expect him to *gnash his teeth* and when he does, moments later, I am as much moved to laughter as fear. He's just as she described him. Just as she *made* him.

Frankenstein.

Victor Frankenstein; that most melodramatic

of characters; the hero and antihero of Mary's abysmal novel.

'I know you,' I say. 'Yes. Yes, I do.'

Frankenstein. Of course, most people these days know that Frankenstein is *not* the name of the monster, but the name of the man who made him. That was not always the case. Very often the lay-reader, or maybe it would be fairer to say cinema-goer, has confused the name of the creator with his creation.

And what is the name of the monster? He does not have one. Victor never gave him one. Or do I mean Mary never gave him one? (And what do we feel towards those who we do not even bother to name? What an act! Dehumanisation, no less.)

'I would not be who she would have me be,' Victor says, and starts to pace the room in a fashion so comical that I would laugh again, were I watching this on the safety of a screen, and not before my eyes. But since it is happening before my eyes, it is. . . unsettling, to say the very least.

'No!' he declares, turning on his heel just before my desk, pacing back towards me. 'I would not be who she would have me be!'

He stands, staring right through me.

'And what would you rather be?' I ask eventually.

He doesn't answer immediately. A moment later, he sinks to both knees, and lowers his head into his palms. When he speaks, it is so softly that I can barely hear.

'She made me a monster.'

That could be taken two ways, I think. At least, but I decide to go with the obvious.

'I have to agree with you,' I say. 'And I hope that doesn't offend you, but—'

'She made me a monster!' he repeats, standing, throwing his arms out wide like the worst amateur dramatician.

I look at the floor, holding up a hand in

apology, again experiencing the weird mixture of the compulsion to laugh and the insipient feeling of fear.

'I—'

'Think on it!' he cries. 'Think on what she made me. At *her* bidding, I made her that creature. She portrays me as noble, as a man above ordinary men; wise and gifted, and yet look what she makes me do. I make her creature; and I call it *her* creature for I wanted no part of it; I make her creature and then her creature becomes a killer. Shunned and hated, it learns to hate as fast as it learns to read!'

I nod. That is true. It reminds me of another thing I find ridiculous about the book: that the monster learns to speak, to read, in fact, to enter into complex philosophical debate, and all by listening through the wall of the cottage where he's hiding, listening to the conversations and readings of the peasant family. Oh, except they're not really a peasant family, are they? No, of course not, they're a *noble* family fallen on hard times, and ill luck, because genuine peasants would never do, would never have the depth of feeling or sensitivity to serve as protagonists in Mary's snobbish tale.

But maybe the fault is mine. The lack of disbelief. I have no problems believing that Victor can compose a living man from the discarded body parts of the charnel house and the rotting bone-yard. Yet I pick holes in other equally improbable events. So is the fault mine? Or is it Mary's for not convincing me with her story? Who holds the ultimate responsibility for the story? The writer or the reader, the reader or the writer. . .

Victor breaks from another reverie and paces the room again.

'Yes,' he says. He stops. 'But none of this is my doing! And what else does she make me? The creature kills! Kills young William, my little brother. Accused of the murder is our maid,

Justine, and though I know she is not guilty, do I do a thing to stop her going to her hanging? I do not! I merely do all I am good for; I wring my hands and bemoan my fate, but do I lift a solitary finger, say even a single word to save her neck from the rope? No!'

He scowls.

He rails and moans, as he draws a hideously painful depiction of himself; by turns he endangers half his family, and his friends too. Henry Clerval dies at the monster's hands, and still Victor says nothing to anyone of what he has done; of why this is his fault.

'Do you find it credible? Could any man be so cold, so callous? Hah! But this is what she would have me be. And there is not a damned thing I can do about it. She has me, for all time. She has me! And I tell you this. I tell you this as sure as I stand before you: my creation follows me, as I follow it. My creation will come, and will come soon!'

I find I do not want to laugh so much any more.

What do they say? Knowledge is knowing that Frankenstein is not the monster in Mary's novel, while wisdom is knowing that Frankenstein *is* the monster in Mary's novel. For Victor is a monster, no two ways about it. He creates a creature that kills the innocent, and does nothing to confess to his errors until it is too late for many innocent people. Yet he wants me to understand something else. At the least, he shares the blame for the actions of his creation with the god who made him, a god by the name of Mary.

But I do not like what he said about his creation following on behind. Something occurs to me, though, something very important.

'Do you think you can be saved?' I ask.

'Do you know me? Do you know me?'

I see what he means, at once. He means he

is what he is, and that he cannot alter from the way he was created. A sudden wave of despair engulfs not just me, but the room itself. He begins to pace in that all-too-familiar manner, and I wonder if he can be helped. Maybe I can help him, maybe it is possible to change your nature, no matter how hard it has been cut into the rock.

'I would not be who she would have me be,' he says, a little more quietly than before. Something is already tickling the back of my brain.

'Yes, I see—' I begin, but he cuts me off.

'No!' he declares, with less vehemence than before. 'I would not be who she would have me be!'

The tickling at the base of my brain is growing more insistent. I try something.

'Where were you born?' I ask. 'In Geneva, I think. Not so far from—'

'She made me a monster!' He cuts across me

and I rise from my chair and circle behind him. He does not follow my movements, not even in the slightest, but stands before the fire.

'Think on it!' he cries. 'Think on what she made me. At her bidding, I made her that creature of mine.'

Now I know for sure. He continues his speech, exactly as it was before, perhaps a touch quieter, and he paces the room, up and down and announces, 'Do you find it credible? Could any man be so cold, so callous?' just as he did before, in fact, every word, word for word, just as he did before, yet more quietly, more quietly, and by the time he reaches the end and stands in front of the fire, looking at nothing, at no one and says, 'Do you know me?' I feel a coldness slide up into my belly and I want to be sick.

I take the chair from my desk, and sit behind him, watching. It is too much to see his face, too much to see, as he goes over his lines, again and again, throws his arms wide, kneels, paces, turns and declaims his melodramatic life, stuck in infinite loops, growing quieter each time, as if someone is slowly turning down the sound on a television set. And then I see that he is starting to fade, this tired ghost. It's the firelight I see through him first; showing through his leg are the flames of the log burner and I know he is going.

It takes an age, maybe an hour or more. An eternity in which he slowly dies before me. It is unbearable to watch, unbearable to hear, but gradually he goes, step by step, word by word; his voice fades and his body fades, until finally, he's gone, and I am left with the final words of his that it was possible to hear.

My creation will come.

S

My creation will come.

I need to get out of here, not just out of this house, but away, gone for good.

Yesterday's snow has vanished, more or less, as fast as it arrived, but I know I have been warned. It will come to stay permanently soon, and I already knew I would have to leave before then. Maybe I have failed, maybe not. I have a few tens of thousands of words done, but I know they are messy, disjointed. I know, with the awful gut ache that tells a writer these things, that they are not yet a *book*. Maybe they can be, maybe not, but I know my time here is over.

I start to gather my things, and there is not much to pack, because I brought very little. I will have to make several trips to the car, but I think I can get it down to three if I leave the unopened tins of food behind.

I stuff my clothes into my larger rucksack and take it to the door, pulling my boots on, crouching on the porch. I hoist the bag on to my back and set off, down from the house, on the track towards the car. An almost ludicrous fear that the car will be gone, or damaged, or unable to start when I get to it grows in me, and I find myself half-jogging the final stretch, only returning to a walk when I see it sitting on the bend, exactly as before, though with a thin sheet of icy snow covering it – a spotless and even blanket left from the fall yesterday.

Wiping the snow from the boot with my forearm, I pop it open and stow my bag. Then I cannot stop myself from getting in and turning the engine over. It starts immediately and I laugh at myself for being so silly as to believe it might not have done. Still, I let it run for a while, warming the engine for a good five minutes till I'm sure it's happy.

I set off back to the house; there's a second bag: that's my bedding. And then there's my other stuff: the laptop, books, papers. I reach the house quickly enough, thinking I must finally be getting used to the lack of air up here, and barge the door open.

I'm halfway across the room when something stops me dead. My rucksack, the one I put in the boot of the car, is sitting in the middle of the rug in front of the fire.

I do nothing.

I mutter one short, bad word under my breath, and my skin starts to itch, feverishly.

I am out of the door again a few moments later, heading to the car with my bag on my back, and it's only when I have been tramping for twenty minutes that I realise I should have reached the car, and that I realise that I'm walking uphill, not down, and that the bag is no longer on my back.

I stop dead, to see where I am; on the track up away from the house, towards the mountain, no, not exactly towards the mountain, because there, a short way through the trees, is that other house.

Turning, I put it behind me, and head back towards *my* house, and the car, but I have gone no more than another fifty paces when I see the other place in front of me. I'm closer this time.

I say the bad word again, and my hands start to shake. But it seems I have no choice, for though I try three more times to walk away from the house, it appears before me again each time.

Once more I swear, and hang my head in despair.

'OK,' I say, and I approach the house.

It's old, at least as old as Étienne's house.

Approaching it from below, it looms out of the closing trees, weighty and enigmatic, majestic. I can see two faces of the house as I come closer: one looks directly down the sloping forest floor, the other, longer, with some kind of opening at ground level. The windows are shuttered. Hammered shut, I now see, as I get closer.

All around the house is junk. Piles of old things: some nameable, some unknowably decomposed. A set of moss-covered concrete steps leads up to the higher side of the house, out of sight.

I take them.

More junk.

Piles of old bottles, lumps of corroding metal. Hundreds of empty tins spilling from bursting boxes. A broken table. Mattresses, that reek of wet and decay from yards distant. There's the main door into the top floor here, but again, it's shuttered tight, as are two more windows; sheets of thin rusting metal have been nailed across all the openings.

I turn the next corner, coming down the far side from where I arrived and see more piles of rubbish. Sheets of corrugated iron, leaning against the wall, dying. Old leather and cardboard suitcases, rotting, like everything else here.

There's a small level area of ground, overgrown with ivy, ferns, weeds but in the middle of it sits the wet residue of a bonfire. Something draws me closer: I lean over the extinct fire pit and see the remains of a shoe. It's hard to be sure, but it looks like a woman's shoe. Then I see another, but it doesn't belong to the first. I peer closer, and now I've started to see them, I easily count the burned remains of at least six different pairs of shoes. Some strips of clothing. A watch strap, old, clearly, but impossible to know how old.

I stand, feeling that familiar fingernail of fear stroking the back of my neck. Something I have clumsily written into a dozen novels strokes down my spine for real.

I continue my tour, down and around to the fourth side of the building. There's a flimsy lean-to tacked on to the back, but nothing else of note, and then I'm at the first side of the house again, where there's the low opening I saw before. It gapes at me. And though I don't want to, I know I have to. I approach.

Inside, to one side, are piles of wood; not nice neat log stacks like everyone makes round here, but a vast mound of splintered crates and spindly branches, heaps of worm-ridden logs and shattered floorboards.

On the other side is a door. I know it must lead into the cellar; the *cave*. It's ancient, and heavy, and into its aging surface things have been scratched, long ago from the look of it. There are clusters of words; in French, and from what I can make out, old French; the writing is cursive and indistinct and I can only decipher the occasional word. There are strange verb forms no longer spoken. There is a date next to one inscription, a date in June, but I cannot see the year. There is a kind of signature at the bottom of one set of lines; ornate: *Ab. . .* I cannot read the rest.

Then there are symbols scratched into the door. Symbols. A simple cross, but which has had a large V-shape etched over it at a later date: I can see that from the different signs of aging. There are other, smaller individual symbols. There's another; it's a triangle, of course. An isosceles triangle, standing on its short side. Inside, along the bottom, are ranged three Xs. Above them a line has been drawn and inside the space left above is a double-barred cross. And then the whole triangle has another simple cross placed at the top, like the cross at the top of a church spire.

I stare at it.

I hear breathing. No.

No, I don't hear breathing, but it's too easy to imagine, too tempting, up here on the bleak face of a lonely mountain, by a dead house in the woods. It's easy to imagine, and it's easy to feel the pressing of thumb and finger across my windpipe.

I stare at the symbols; the triangular one holds me most. The three Xs in it remind me of something: Sigmund Freud and Carl Jung used to put three small crosses in their letters to each other whenever they mentioned something superstitious, or fearful, or merely an irreverent idea. It was a private joke between them, and I remember that they took it from old barns and houses in the Alps, places just like this; the three crosses were to ward off ill-luck and evil.

I decide to leave.

Ducking out of the low opening to the space by the cellar door, I take a few steps. I hear a noise behind me; a crack, like someone stepping on dry wood. I spin; but of course there is nothing to be seen. The house glares at me, and now I see something I'd missed before.

Painted on the side, in large but fading yellowish letters, is a single word.

'Oh, Christ,' I say aloud, though quietly, for I

do not want to disturb anyone, or anything, for I can sense that there is something here. I sense that very powerfully indeed.

Painted on the house is what can only be its name.

Piège.

Simultaneously, I remember what it means.

It means *trap.*

E

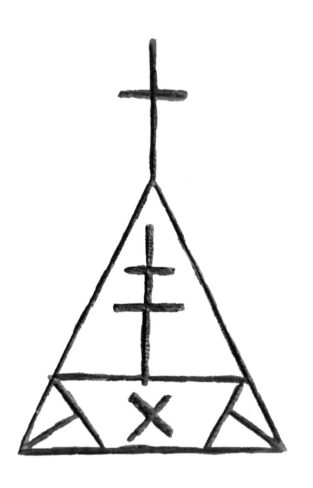

My creation will come.

   My creation will come.

   My creation will...

I tried to walk back to the car so many times I lost count. Walking in circles, maybe, or maybe in triangles.

The chalet *Piège* had let me go, sure enough, then, but it seemed only to permit me back as far as my home of these recent weeks, still exerting its weird pull on me.

There sat my rucksack, as I had left it by the fire. And all my things stacked and ready to go on my desk. And a fire burning in both the pot-belly and the log burner; fires that I had not lit.

'Oh,' I said. 'Oh. Holy Christ.'

All things come in threes. Any writer worth their words will tell you that; in fact, any *reader* can tell you that, because we like things to come in threes. Especially in stories – three wishes, three trolls, three guesses – but we expect them in real life too. As if stories are not real life! Of course stories are real life – they are made by living beings, not machines, and the day that a machine can tell a decent story is the day we should dig a six foot hole in the ground, gently lay ourselves down inside it and let the falling soil cover our faces and take us away.

One is a point. Two is a line. Only with three do we start to feel the strength of physical space.

Huh, I think then, *the triangle*.

I am here because of triangulation, after all. I am here because of triangulation. After all.

Trapped within this triangle, I wait for my third visitor, Victor's creation.

I think about horror. I have contributed enough horror to the world, I know. With my books. With one book, in particular, the one that brought me fame, and money, where all the others I had written had done nothing more than sit in warehouses, unsold, unread, unloved, or in library stacks with a solitary return-date stamped inside the cover, if any.

I want to put all that behind me, because the world has horrors enough of its own, don't you think? And yes, I know what I was doing – writing is a way, a very, very good way of understanding the world, both the good and wonderful things and the awful things too, and that's why I had written horror – not to scare people. It was never about that, never, whatever I found it simpler to say on the stage at book festivals. No, it was something else, something else entirely. It was just to say, *Look! I'm scared by this. Should you not be scared too?*

And finally people were scared by that book; the one I wrote, ten years ago or more, which sold as easily as the water voids itself down the reverberating chasm beneath the house.

It just will not stay on the shelves! they told me, grinning, thinking of the money. And I grinned back, thinking of the glory. And my nasty little secret.

I did what I did and I cannot undo that now. At least it brought me security, for a good while, if not forever, and as the years have turned over, I started to know it brought me something else – the desire to leave the horror behind. For there is both horror in the world, and beauty, and I wish to turn to that. Yet every writer worth a good-god damn knows this too, for it is graven into each of us: no one cares for beauty. Not in fiction. Not on its own, not pure, untroubled beauty; not in *fiction*. It's what we crave in the real world, of course; beauty, and you know I mean that in its broadest sense: the sense of kindness and wisdom and peace and joy: all the things in the world that are beautiful, and all the things we crave in real life, but which are not sufficient to count, on their own, for anything in the world of stories.

For here is the only real difference between the life of reality and the life of fiction. Fiction only works when the beauty is tainted by pain. For fiction is not about life; it's about *the troubles* in life. That is why we read it. To understand, to grow, to know, to believe, to hope. That all the troubles one faces in life can be overcome, eventually.

Or not. And that's when horror writing is its most horrific; when it turns to you, the reader, and with a leer on its face, says, *No. There is no happy ending this time.*

I'm sitting in the chair, waiting.

A while ago, as darkness fell, I took a torch to the door and played it out into the night, daring whatever is coming to come, and be damned. But the pale torchlight showed nothing but the descent of a million, million flakes of snow, falling soft and untroubled.

They're still falling, smothering everything without urgency, without anger, without judgement, without ego, as if they know they have all the time in the world in which to complete their task of hiding everything that mankind ever knew.

My creation will come.

I hear breathing. Not in the air around me, but in my mind, breathing, slow breathing, breathing, and the pressing of a finger and thumb of gigantic size against my throat, gently, gently pressing.

And then I must have slept once more, by the fireside once more, because when I wake, a young woman is standing in front of me.

R

My creation will come.

So Victor said, yet that is not what I see before me now, but a young woman, a woman I have already met, in fact; it is Mary, I have no doubt. But she is young, maybe just eighteen or nineteen. At most twenty, I'm sure: the age when she published her book.

She seems very different from the imposing lady I spoke to before, immediately I can tell that, though I cannot place what it is. One small thing: I notice that the locket is no longer around her neck, and I presume it has not yet been fashioned. Perhaps Percy is not yet dead, for this Mary. Blessed are the eyes that saw him alive.

She looks down at me, but there is none of the cool hostility I felt from her older self. Then, she was that unspoken power that threatens without need for words or action, but simply states its power through its boldness alone. *If I can carry this burden, I have no fear of you.* And what burdens she carried, what painful burdens, all those years. Now, Mary seems to be merely waiting for me, for me to be something or do something, perhaps just to wake up.

I rouse myself, and stand, and not for the first time I tell myself that this isn't happening, that none of this is happening, because it cannot be. Yet events seem to be ignoring what I have to say about them. And there is nothing to do but play along, taking the role of the pawn.

I offer her the seat by the fire, but she shakes her head, slowly, and holds her weaker arm out, her wrist slightly hanging, as she indicates the corner of the room where the door to the hidden floor of the house stands ajar.

'Please?' she says, and it is not a threat but I know it is not really a question either. I nod, and make my way to the stairs, thinking she must have vanished again for her footsteps make no sound, but when I turn she is disconcertingly close, right behind me, so close on my heels that I hurry down the steps into the darkness.

'The first room, if you please.' She gestures and I turn the corner. A light is coming from the room which held the only piece of furniture across the whole of this floor of the house; the little round table with the key lying inside the drawer. As I enter, I see there are now two chairs next to the table, and a decrepit oil lamp, alight on its surface.

She indicates the chairs, and I wonder if I am supposed to take one rather than the other; whether it will matter which I sit on.

She solves the problem by taking the chair on the right of the table, I join her on the left.

She says nothing, and a long silence empties itself into the shadows, so long that I know she is waiting for me to begin.

'I. . . I was expecting something, someone, else,' I say.

She smiles, but it's a weak smile, that says more about desperation than happiness.

I wonder if she knows we met before, when

she was her older self. Or is this young Mary innocent of that? Through my mind I run what snippets of her life I can recall. At this point, what had she lost? One child? Two? Is her husband dead yet? No, not quite, but it will not be long. And her husband's estranged wife. . . she will soon throw herself into the Serpentine, drowned, like Percy himself. And Mary's half-sister, there is not long to live before she will swallow those pills. I try to read any of this real-life horror on Mary's face; but I can't see anything.

'You mean the creature,' she says in reply.

I nod.

'Victor said his creation would follow him. . .'

'And Victor was right. Our creations follow us, whether we like it or not. I know you are aware of that yourself. Are you not?'

This again. She means the book. My book. My *successful* book.

She continues.

'And just as our creations follow us, so they also start to say something about us, in return. They begin to define us. I sense that you are also aware of this?'

And, *My god*, I think, *that's true*. I wrote that book, and I thought I was in control. Hah! How absurd is that? And how vain! Because as soon as it was done, and in the world, and began to be read and talked about and read, it was no longer in my control. And even more than that, it started to define *me*, in return. As a writer, even as a person, perhaps, because people know me as the writer of that book, and nothing more. Nothing more. How much worse it must have been for Mary! She whose first novel became one of the world's most famous works of literature, almost overnight. From the moment of its birth, her novel must have created *her*, as much as *she* had created *it*. It will have taken its toll, no doubt. Maybe its revenge.

'I see you understand me,' she says. 'It's true.

I am as much made by the book I wrote and the characters I created, as by who I was myself. Since Victor is part of the book, I am now as much his creation, as he was originally mine.'

This conversation is starting to unsettle me. I try for the last time to talk myself out of it; but give it up. From here on I know I can only watch myself. No more than that.

He was born just a few years before Mary died, so perhaps she doesn't know that Nietzsche put his finger on it: *Whoever fights monsters should see to it that in the process he does not himself become a monster.* If what we make comes back to haunt us, to define us and alter us, well, then, hadn't we better be very careful what we create? Snatches of the things I have created in my books irrupt into my mind, and I suddenly fear their presence in my life, eating at me from the inside. *If you gaze into an abyss for long enough, the abyss will gaze back into you.* What if these things were to come back to haunt me?

And then, with a cold sickness, I realise that they already have. Like the virus of inspiration, they are in me already; changing me, colouring my view of the world, perhaps preventing me from ever finding peace, or joy; because what I wrote was *horror*.

Fast on that thought comes another.

'We are responsible for our creations,' I say, and with that she lifts a finger rapidly into the light of the lamp, and only now do I notice the subtle smell that I take to be the oil, mineral and dead. Mineral and dead, something quite like gas, and I am aware that I am being pulled in closer to Mary, to Mary's world.

'Yes!' she declares. 'Now you have it. Now you approach the truth.'

She seems to have more in her, so I stay silent, until she finds a way to begin.

'I believe I told you,' she says (and I see that she does know that she's spoken to me before), 'that from the start, my book has been misunderstood.

From the moment of its issue into the world, it has been cast as something it is not. Are you aware of this?'

I am, and I tell her so.

Ask most people what the message of *Frankenstein* is, and they will tell you one of two things. They may perhaps say that it's a book about the dangers of playing God. Victor meddles with occult science that he should leave well alone, and the result is evil, horror. Death. Or perhaps, in a more modern take, you might have someone tell you it's about the dangers of science itself; how we like to think that science is always benign, whereas the truth is that science leads to as much destruction and damnation as it does advancement.

'But,' I say, 'with respect, you may have yourself to blame for this.'

She bristles slightly but inclines her head to direct me to explain.

'Your subtitle. *The Modern Prometheus.*

Prometheus stole the secrets of fire and learning from the gods, and was punished by them as a result. It's no wonder people felt that way about your book since you called Victor Frankenstein "Prometheus" in your subtitle.'

She closes her eyes. Nods slowly, once.

'Perhaps,' she says. She waits with her eyes still closed for a long time, as if remembering painful things, until finally she rouses herself.

'But, you know, there are even blunter falsifications that have been foisted upon it – those laughable interpretations of my book on the stage, for example.'

And on the cinema screen, I add, but I wonder if she even knows about such things. The moving pictures – in film versions of Mary's novel, Victor unwittingly puts the brain of a murderer in his creature, and so it's born evil.

The first was James Whale, Hollywood, 1931. No, wait. It returns to me that there was a short film before that, an even earlier one.

1910! Yes, 1910. A twelve-minute long adaptation of Mary's story, depicting the creation of the monster. And yes, even there, he was born a monster. He does not become one later as happens in the novel; he is born evil. And why? The audience is told that 'the evil in Frankenstein's mind creates a monster'. *A liberal adaptation*, it was called. So very liberal.

'Yes,' Mary is saying, 'the very first adaptation of my book; on stage, which I myself saw in 1823; and already this mistaken notion about what my story actually is.'

'How so?' I ask.

'The very title of the piece tells you all you need to know: it is called *Presumption; or, The Fate of Frankenstein.*'

'Playing God, again,' I say. 'Playing God settles your fate. A bad one.'

'Quite,' Mary says.

'But, if I remember rightly from the biographies, you did not entirely hate this play.'

She fixes me with a look and I see a glimpse of her fifty-three-year-old self from her previous visit.

'Indeed. But in time I have come to learn that by then, my creation was already out of my hands. From its origin, the meaning I wanted people to take from the book was missed, while these other messages were set in its place. And you know, maybe even I did not know what my book really meant. Not till later, long after it was out in the world.'

That makes sense to me. Sometimes we write and we know what we do. But mostly, I suspect, we don't. Mary stands, and takes a slow turn around the table while she speaks, her fingers trailing in the dust on the table top, the lace on the hem of her dress sweeping the boards. I notice her footsteps make no sound; no trace appears of her fingertips in the dust.

'People say it is about the dangers of playing God. This is not true. Nowhere in the text will you find words denouncing Victor's attempts to create life. People say it is about the dangers of modern science. Yet nowhere in the text will you find this idea to be reinforced – the only thing criticised is that Victor gets his science *wrong* with his misshapen, hideous being, not that he erred by attempting his experiment in the first instance.'

I follow Mary as she turns behind my back, then catch her as she comes into my sight again.

'And so?' I ask. 'The real meaning of the book?'

'Why, you have already given it, just a few moments ago.'

I understand.

'We are responsible for our creations.'

'Exactly correct. This is what Victor's true crime is; not that he creates a man, but that, having created one, he does not care for what he has created. He finds it ugly and repulsive. He shuns it just as people, throughout history, have shunned the poor, or the leper, or the deformed.

Thus, rejected and abandoned, the creature learns the evil ways of man rather than the noble ones. And that is how a monster is born.'

She stands in front of me for a moment, then resumes her tour around the table, into the darkness, behind my back, round again. Each time she turns behind me, I expect her to vanish. She is as silent as an empty room, she may already have gone.

But she speaks.

'It is a book about motherhood. More generally, parenthood. It is about abandonment. The crime of forsaking our offspring. Bringing someone into the world and then casting them adrift. That is the true horror of my book.'

I remember Mary's story a little further. I remember her children.

At the time her book was published, she had lost one baby, a girl, premature at seven months, dying a few days into life. A short time later, Percy and she named their second child William.

I have always found it remarkable...No, I have always found it truly terrifying that, knowing what pain it is to lose a child, she then gave the name of William to Victor's baby brother in her novel, and made him the first victim of the monster's hands. What folly! Or what bravery! Or maybe some awful scratching mischief, as when you do something you know it would be better not to do; like sliding a fingernail under a scab...I have written some horror in my time, yet I could never name a murdered child after one of my children, for fear of hexing them. Of course, nothing would happen. Nothing. Probably. But what if it did? *What if it did?*

I wonder what Mary came to feel about it; given that, eighteen months after the publication of her book, her own William, her real son, was to die, at less than four years of age. Mary would be a mother again; in all three of her four children would die. Motherhood, parenthood, she's right. That's what *Frankenstein* is about; and when we give birth to something, well, shouldn't we love them and care for them whether they live to be a hundred, or die a few days out from the womb?

I watch her as she walks around me, and I know that she knows all this, even though, at the age she has chosen to appear to me, William's death has not yet happened. I know this because, as I wonder these things, she answers me.

'No, I would not name another ill-starred character after my child, were I have to have my chances over again.'

She pauses.

'So, you are going to assist me, are you not?'

I hate this book. I wanted to destroy it, for all its flaws and snobbery, I wanted to pour scorn on it. But she's right, I am going to help her, for she wrote something powerful that was taken out of her hands the moment it was born, through which her own meaning has been lost.

Therefore, I have nothing to do, but stand, put my hand out as she offers me hers, and I say, 'Yes.'

Our skin touches, for a second, maybe two, as we seal our deal, and I wonder if the skin I am touching is alive or dead and I wonder whether I am still alive, or dead.

She smiles, briefly, and bids me sit down in the chair again.

She retakes her seat.

The light from the lamp flickers and glows and her face is not the face of a long dead woman but a girl of little more than teenage years. Thus it is disconcerting when she slides open the drawer, and lifts out the key, with the label.

'You know where this belongs now?'

'The cellar of *Le Piège*, I presume.'

'And you know what is in there?'

I swallow.

'I do.'

'You must not let him out. Not yet. Not as he is. At the moment, at the moment, there is the monster that everyone imagines my creature to be. He must not go out into the world again in this form. You have to recreate him. That is your task. You have to stay here and recreate him as he originally was. Not evil, but innocent. A blank canvas, on to which the best of human life might have been bestowed. This is your chance.'

'How? Do you mean I am to rewrite your book?'

Once more she stands and circles me.

'I. . . I am not sure how it can be done. That is for you to decide. I have faith. You have to find a way to recreate my book, if not rewrite it. But there is one matter above all else. . .'

'Yes?'

She turns behind me, out of sight in the murky room.

'You must have people understand this: that we are responsible for what we create.'

'But, I cannot... I mean, I don't know if it's even possible to—'

I stop.

I stop, because she has gone, and I am talking to the dark, empty air. The lantern burns. The snow falls.

V

monster (n.)

early 14c., "malformed animal or human, creature afflicted with a birth defect"

from Old French monstre, mostre "monster, monstrosity" (12c.)

and directly from Latin monstrum "divine omen, portent, sign; abnormal shape; monster, monstrosity"

figuratively "repulsive character, object of dread, awful deed, abomination"

from root of monere "to admonish, warn"

from proto-Indo-European *moneyo-, suffixed (causative) form of root *men- "to think"

To think.
    Monster means to *think*.
    A monster means to think.
    So all our thoughts are monsters?

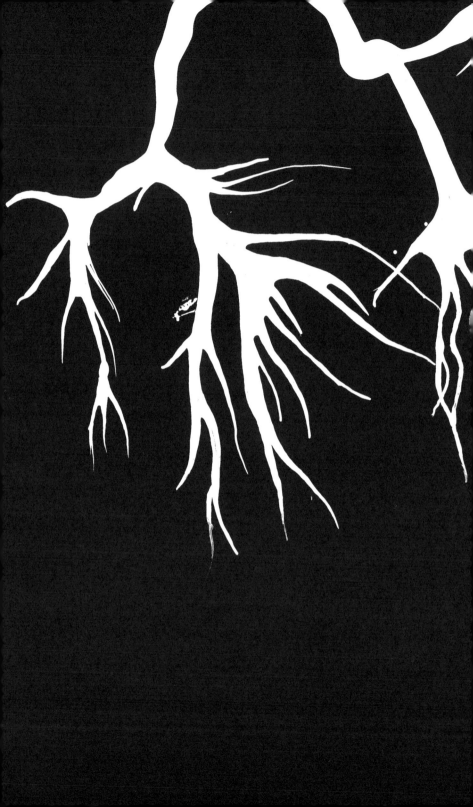

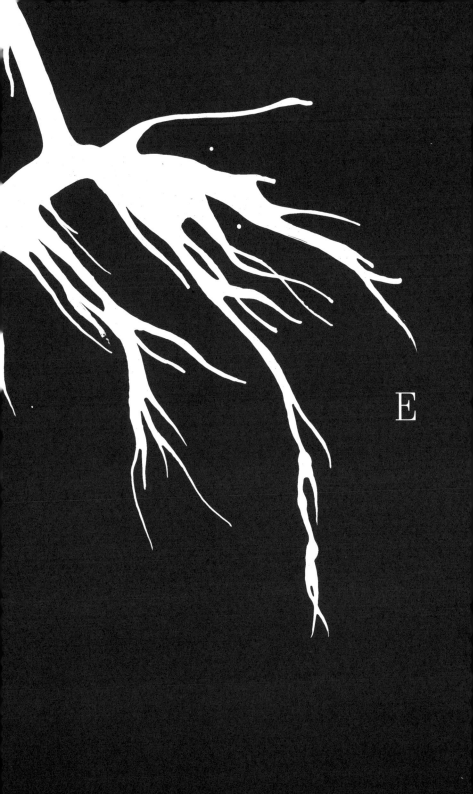

E

Trapped.

Unable to leave, unable to write. For how can I possibly achieve what she wants me to achieve? I find I want to help her, I do. But it's an impossible task, isn't it? To change the past?

Maybe. Maybe not. History can be rewritten. That happens sometimes; when one ideology supplants another, when what were the facts are re-cast, discarded and remade, for 'new' facts. That is why books get burned, by those who would rewrite not just history, but an entire culture. And now Mary wants me to burn her book. So it can be remade, and yet, as I said, books cannot be burned, as long as they are alive in one person's memory. Yet perhaps there is a slim chance that I can do what she wants me to. And if I can, I want to, for I see now why I need to myself. I have to believe we can be something other than the thing we have created, and in order to believe it, I need to see it happen.

I presume I am out of time, now. I mean, *outside* of time. That nothing can touch me, and that nothing can get to me.

I do not stay in the hidden floor of the house, but return to the living room where the fire burns.

Through the grimy window I can just see the ghosts of falling flakes, still unhurried, still steady and strong.

If I am outside of time, I wonder whether the snow will fall forever, entombing me in a white mountain, of purity and silence. Will food keep appearing in my cupboards? Will that final bottle of wine I have been saving continually reappear on the worktop, even though I may drain it dry every night? Will there even be night and day, or just this one infinite night of snowfall?

It seems probable. It seems probable in the way that Victor and his monster chase each other across the Arctic wastes at the end of the novel, even though, as Victor dies, the creature announces he will travel on till he finds a place to build a funeral pyre and throw himself into the flames.

Victor did not die. The creature did not immolate himself. Both still live in the pages of Mary's book and in our minds, locked in an eternal duel for mastery over the other. That is the power of the book. Immortality, for better, or worse. It is majestic, in its way, this immortality. And powerful. Once a story is started, once a lie is told, it is very difficult to un-tell it, and yet this is what Mary would have me do.

I. . .

I must find a way, then, to—

I must find a way to do what must be done. So I. . .

When a writer sets out to create something new, when she, or he, makes a monster, does—

Does it mean that when a writer makes a

monster, who is the... that is, when a writer makes, makes, a monster, does he or she...?

Settle. I need to settle for a while, and I have time if I am out of time. All the time I need. I could let days pass and maybe just breathe once, or twice. I could let the moon calendar itself through the sky and put just one word on paper. Then cross it out again. I have time.

Calm yourself.

Here's the thing. When a writer makes a monster, who is the real monster? The monster, or the writer who made it? I start to move to something here, and I – I move to my desk, and bring my things over. To work.

I must settle to this work. Of creating a monster. No! Of recreating a creature in its true image. A man. Just a simple man, born not exactly as a baby, but certainly like a child, ready to learn, ready to absorb whatever is put before it. A creature that could be the best of us, not the worst.

Where to start?

I remember that there was that time. . .

No. That's not—

Here's another thought. *Mary knows.* Mary knows what I did. My book. Not hers. The thing that drives me crazy, if I let it (and I often do).

She knows, she knew. She knew from the start what I did, she knew everything about me, more than anyone, more than me myself, and while outside the snow falls, inside I am taken back to the time I wrote that book, and I shudder.

Maybe what I did was not so bad, not by some people's standards. I did not murder anyone. I did not hurt anyone but myself, and another writer, a man long gone into history. But what I did has hurt me more than I could have believed at the time. I was not to know that that book, *that book*, would be the one to bring me money, and the modest fame of the writer. Of all the others, I could say volumes, but there they sat on the warehouse shelves, boxed, while the book that made me the writer I am – the book that *created me*, flew out of bookshops as fast as they could print it.

And what was it I did?

I stole.

I stole something – I stole the plot for the book. And why? Not even because I couldn't come up with one, not because I had writer's block, not because I was unable to sort out events of my own making. Why then? For a joke. For a piece of arrogance that easily matches anything Mary put in her novel. The arrogant belief that people are so ill-read these days that I could steal the plot of a classic novel, and no one would know. I chose a book, a famous book, the sort that everyone says they've read because they 'know they're supposed to'.

But haven't.

Not you, o my publisher.

Not the editors who worked on the book.

Not my agent, not the critics, not the reviewers,

and not the readers. That was my arrogant claim, and you know? I was proved right. All along the way, I expected to be caught, and with every gate that the book passed through undetected, the harder it was to confess. And then the book was being published, and the rest, well, you know the rest.

So my success is a lie. It's based on a theft. And it leaves me hollow, and wondering if I have any right to call my success by that name at all.

We are responsible for our creations.

And our creations end up creating us, in return. Create a lie, and you become one.

I know I—

I ought to. I mean, I ought to make...

There's snow falling. And I see that time has unravelled to the point at which it is without meaning. Did I leave the lantern alight downstairs? I can't remember and I know I ought to check, but the door to the stairs is shut tight.

Won't open.

I put my hand in my pocket and snow is falling and the key is not in my pocket. The key is not in any of my pockets because the key is in the drawer of the small round table downstairs in the hidden rooms. I will need that key. I will need that key, but only when the creature has been re-cast.

I have to—

There's a sound now. And I know what it is. Breathing. It's breathing, breathing and I feel the push and squeeze of a fingertip and a thumb on my throat. My throat, emptying, no, my mind is not coping with—

I wake with a start, I fall asleep by the fire.

Cold.

The fire is cold. I light it. I sense the smell of something, something mineral and long dead. Or living still? And something is nearby, not inside the house. But nearby, something is very close, breathing, breathing, breathing. Then.

Stops.

And then. I search.

I see myself searching.

Writing.

Doing.

Being.

Being very little more than nothing as time winds out and then I hear that breathing again, right outside, right outside the damn door. There is the smell of gas. A shadow is thrown across my mind. I run.

Run.

No, walk, torch, and then throwing the door wide there's the snow falling; the night, the trees, and the snow is very thick upon the ground and in the snow is a trail; footprints.

The snow is transforming the forest, transforming the world. Somewhere in the night the stag stands under the boughs of a pine, the burden of its antlers weighing it down but when the winter comes it will lose them, transformed to something new. A different kind of beast then? No. No, the animal remains.

Still, footprints.

Footprints.

Stare at them.

Up to the door, fresh; you can see the crispness of their outline already softening with the falling snow. Someone was here, right here, a moment ago. Calling. To me. I know I can do nothing but follow. Such an overwhelming call. I tremble as I get ready, hands shaking, skin crawling, my heart thumps.

The torch.

Coat, big coat.

Boots.

Gloves, I will need gloves.

And the torch, the torch, I shake it, and go out into the night.

Footprints deep, knee-deep.

And it's slow but I follow them, alongside them, making my way, I have to follow. The torchlight flashes white crystals into my path, diamonds on the snow (remember that?) diamonds, millions of beautiful and worthless diamonds that lead me up, away from the house, towards the centre of the world, the very centre of the triangle, I know where that is now, it's the trap ahead of me, but I have to see who it is who's leading me there, I have to move fast in the thick snow.

Away. House behind, forest ahead.

I push on. Breathing, breathing.

Minute after minute now. Panting. The gloves are loose and I stop to pull them and snow from the branch of a tree falls down my neck, and I stagger on, on.

Then.

There it is. The trap. Waiting.

Piège.

It's hunkered (and why is that word any better?) into the deepening snow, and the footprints lead up and up towards it, and I know I must hurry, because that thing must not be let out again, not as it is. I see that now. Mary is right. Mary, my Mary. We are both as trapped as each other. I cannot hate her book any more. Her tale, her fairy tale. I can only pity it as I pity myself, with my own cheap deceptions. And I pity her too, with her cry for a better ending to her fairy tale.

Floundering. Falling. Falling *again*. Towards the trap, and the opening in the side, still clear enough of snow to make my way under and then. . .

Breathing. I can hear it, from the other side of the cellar door, breathing so slow.

Deep.

Heavy.

Fingertip and thumb tighten on my windpipe and I can only hear the breathing, I check the door is shut, shut tight. Tight. It's shut tight. Good.

But things unloosen. I'm hanging on for dear life on the side of the dark mountain and here I am in the centre of the world, in the middle of nowhere, and on the other side of an ageing piece of wood is a monster, breathing.

It's hard. So very difficult. I see. . . No, I don't see anything but the snow, triangles, and feel the house around me, and beyond the door. . .

No. All around me. . .

Breathing.

When did I come here? What did I do? Did Mary find me or did I find Mary? Everything is hard now, everything so hard to think straight, just to think straight for one stupid second, so I know what is what. And I smell something in my presence and there is no doubt that something has forced its way into—

Forced its way into me.

All around: blowing snow and the symbols; triangles on the wood, and the pile of sticks. There's a date. Writing and a date on the door, and the door is open. The door is *open* and inside is darkness and breathing.

Push my way in, torch flashing, this way,

that. . . There's nothing, nothing but breathing filling me, filling me, and the torch won't even illuminate a foot in front of me; the darkness absorbs all its light and some of mine.

Then I turn, and I see it.

Just for a moment, bearing down on me, coming out of the dark. Its face is a shocking apology on which is written its whole story. Every ugly weeping bare muscle that twitches around its eyes, every drawn sinew in its neck describes to me the futility of what Mary wants. And I know that we cannot control the things we create, because people believe what they want to believe. They take what they want from what they read, and what they see, and it matters not one tiny bit if that is not what was intended. And if the idea that they want to believe is actually more powerful than the idea that was created, then yes, that is the idea that will survive. That will be selected. It is natural.

I know Mary's task is futile. My task is futile. We get the monsters we deserve, and there is nothing Mary or I can do about it.

There is only the creature, forever. There is no fairy tale, ending.

The creature towers above me, looming, the back of its naked skull rubbing against the low ceiling of the cellar. It lowers its face, close to mine, and with its seeping eyes, inspects me for three long seconds. I feel the press of fingertip and thumb upon my throat, and its breath on my face, in my nostrils, in my lungs, where crystals of ice have lodged themselves and will never melt. Without saying a word, the creature speaks:

> *If I can carry this burden, I need have no fear of you. Nor anyone.*

I close my eyes, and wait for it to annihilate me.

Then I hear movement, and opening my eyes see it turn, and stride away. Away. It sets out into the world once more.

I follow it to the threshold, still grasping the torch in one hand, shining my feeble light after it. Already, it is invisible, part of the darkness of the night.

My other hand, my cut hand, throbs; and I feel something, I feel something in it, and I look down and see it is the key. The key to this place, this trap.

Then I look at the footprints that brought me here, and I see they were my own.

WE GET THE MONS

At Zephyr we are proud to publish books you can read and re-read time and time again because they tell a brilliant story and because they entertain you.

That's why we've launched the Zephyr Review Crew. We'd like to hear about the things you love in our books and what you think we could do better.

Join our review crew and be the first to read the very best new books. Members will receive exclusive author content and chances to win signed books. Just drop us a line at *hello@headofzeus.com*

 @HoZ_Books

HeadofZeus

WWW.READZEPHYR.COM

ZEPHYR

Tomorrow's classics today